The
Buenos Aires
Affair

The Buenos Aires Affair

A DETECTIVE NOVEL

Manuel Puig

TRANSLATED BY SUZANNE JILL LEVINE

VINTAGE BOOKS
A DIVISION OF RANDOM HOUSE
NEW YORK

FIRST VINTAGE BOOKS EDITION, August 1980
Copyright © 1974 by Manuel Puig.
English translation copyright © 1976 by E.P. Dutton & Co., Inc.
All rights reserved under International and Pan-American
Copyright Conventions.
Published in the United States by Random House, Inc.,
New York and simultaneously in Canada by Random House of
Canada Limited, Toronto. Originally published by E.P. Dutton
& Co., Inc., New York, in April 1976.

Assistance for the translation of this volume was given by the
Center for Inter-American Relations.

Library of Congress Cataloging in Publication Data
Puig, Manuel.
The Buenos Aires affair.
Reprint of the 1976 1st ed. published by
Dutton, New York.
I. Title.
[PZ4.P9786Bu 1980]   [PQ7798.26.U4]   863   80-11865
ISBN 0-394-74474-8

Manufactured in the United States of America

Part One

I

The handsome young man: You're killing yourself.

Greta Garbo: (feverish, trying to hide her fatigue) If I am, you're the only one who objects, now why don't you go back and dance with one of those pretty girls. Come, I'll go with you, what a child you are (she gives him her hand).

The handsome young man: Your hand's so hot.

Greta Garbo: (ironic) Is that why you put tears on it, to cool it?

The handsome young man: I know I don't mean anything to you, I don't count. But someone ought to look after you, and I could . . . if you let me.

Greta Garbo: Too much wine has made you sentimental.

The handsome young man: It wasn't wine that made me come here every day, for months, to find out how you were.

Greta Garbo: No, that couldn't have been wine. So, you'd really like to take care of me?

The handsome young man: Yes.

Greta Garbo: All day . . . every day?

The handsome young man: All day . . . every day, why not?

Greta Garbo: Why should you care for a woman like me,
I'm always nervous or sick, . . . sad . . . or too gay.

(from *Camille*, Metro-Goldwyn-Mayer)

White Beach, May 21, 1969

A pale winter sun lighted the place in question. The mother woke up a little before seven, certain that nobody was watching her. Instead of getting up she stayed in bed an hour longer so as not to make noise, her daughter was sleeping in the next room and needed sleep as much as or more than food. The mother said the same thing to herself as she said every morning: in her old age she was forced to face serious problems all on her own. Her name was Clara Evelia, but now nobody called her Clarita, the way her deceased husband and parents had always done.

For a few seconds a shadow fell across one of the windows, perhaps the trees in the garden had moved with the wind, but Clara Evelia didn't pay attention, distracted by the thought that atheists like her lacked the comfort of a final reunion with their loved ones now dead, ". . . the lady sleeps! Oh, may her sleep,/ Which is so enduring, so be deep!/ Heaven have her in its sacred keep!"

She got up, put on her warm slippers and looked for a second at her thick wool bathrobe, frayed along the edges, before slipping into it: her daughter got depressed every time she saw her in that threadbare garment. Clara hoped at least for good weather that morning, or more precisely, for it not to rain, so that they could go for a walk on the seaside promenade.

She raised the Venetian blinds and gazed upward, from her memory another stanza surged forth, "strange is thy pallor! strange thy dress!/ Strange above all, thy length of tress,/ And this . . . this . . . this all solemn silentness! . . ." Each time she managed to effortlessly remember a piece from her repertoire Clara Evelia felt somewhat comforted, she had taught elocution for so many years, ". . .

4

above the closed and fringed lid/ 'Neath which thy slumb'ring soul lies hid,/ That, o'er the floor and down the wall,/ Like ghosts the shadows . . . the shadows . . . the shadows . . . the shadows rise and fall!"

The sky was cloudy, but that was common during the winter at White Beach, a small seaside resort on the South Atlantic. It's not going to rain, she thought relieved: during the night she had heard her daughter complain in her sleep, and if because of bad weather she would have to stay inside the whole day it would take time for her to recover. But was there any possible recovery for Gladys? Barely a month ago Clara had thought her cured and now she again saw Gladys at the bottom of that dark aquarium in which she sank, a new and acute nervous breakdown. Which did not necessarily imply a future and total loss of reason, the mother repeated to herself.

The arts, her daughter was an artist, like herself, both too sensitive, Clara Evelia concluded ". . . oh, lady dear, hast thou no fear?/ Why and what are thou dreaming here?/ Sure thou art come o'er far-off seas,/ A wonder to . . . A wonder to . . ." how did those lines continue? she only remembered that those that followed were painful words. As if from afar she seemed to hear a voice, from where did it come? It could barely pierce the glass of the window and the gauze curtain. Clara remained still a moment but heard nothing further. Neither could she remember the rest of the poem.

Irritated she quickly reviewed her successive misfortunes: the death of her husband, her only daughter's long stay in North America, the reduced buying power of her pension, the phone call from the doctors in New York, her return home with a sick Gladys. But she had also received unexpected help, that house, for example, which wealthy friends had offered without her asking. A quiet place by the sea, several months of rest and relaxation had changed Gladys, but a few weeks back in the turmoil of Buenos Aires' artistic circles had been enough to bring her down to zero again.

And they would begin at zero again if necessary, the sky wasn't as grey as it had been a moment before, the color of the sea was undefined although very dark, "far in the forest, dim and old,/ For her may some tall vault unfold —/ Some sepulchre, remote, alone,/ Against whose portal she hath thrown,/ In childhood, many an idle stone—" She decided that a walk would do both of them a lot of good, they would go down to the beach bundled up and with kerchiefs on their heads, being careful not to step in the wet sand, walking along the bushes that hold the dunes in place with their strong roots, "some tomb from out whose sounding door/ She ne'er shall force an echo more,/ thrilling to think, poor child of sin! It was the dead who . . . the dead who . . . ," Clara once again tried to concentrate and during that moment in which she closed her eyes someone could have entered the room without her noticing him. She only remembered that she had slept badly during the night, disturbed by strange noises.

In any case she would take a walk with her daughter, the important thing was to get some exercise and fresh air. She untied the belt of her bathrobe to tie it again, in a bow, and gently knocked on Gladys' door. There was no answer. The mother was content, deep sleep was always healthy, in general her daughter was such a light sleeper that any noise would wake her up, was she getting better? ". . . strange is thy pallor! strange thy dress!/ Strange above all, thy length of tress,/ and this all solemn silentness!," extraordinary lines! she would include them in the festival which she was programming for that winter in White Beach. Months before her daughter had begged her practically on her knees not to recite, but with the crisis over Clara would risk disappointing the convalescent and organize a festival, ". . . my love, she sleeps! oh, may her sleep,/ As it is lasting, so be deep!," Gladys' deep sleep was a sign of quick recovery and the mother felt on her back two strong wings ready to unfold, while something sweet seemed to slip down her throat. Suddenly her wings folded, an electric shock went through her body, in a manner of speaking, and her mouth tasted of the metals that high voltage wires are made of: the white gleam—of a flashlight?—pointed to a detail on the floor so that she wouldn't overlook it. The light went out, and yet muddy footsteps could be seen—from men's shoes?—, already dry they went from the front door, crossing the living room, to her daughter's bedroom door, and back. The gleam of a flashlight seemed to have focused for a moment upon the revealing detail.

Without hesitation Clara opened the bedroom door, the bed was in disorder and Gladys had disappeared. But surely she must have left a message, a few lines saying that she had gone out to look at the sea? The mother looked on the bureau, on the night table, in the drawers, under the bed, in the living room, in the kitchen, to no avail.

Who had entered during the night? The thought of an assault gave her the chills: impossible, Clara herself had bolted the door, Gladys was very cautious and wouldn't have opened it for a stranger. She raised her hand to her temples and dropped onto the couch, why was she getting so frightened? the winter before Gladys had often gotten up at dawn to gather the objects that are left on the sand at ebbtide. But in those cases she never failed to wake up her mother before going out. The mother stood up, did not look to her right—where she might have noticed an unexpected presence—and ran to the bathroom to look for the basket where Gladys always put the flotsam that she gathered. She prayed not to find it, but the basket was there. She returned to the living room repeating the same course in the opposite direction, for fortuitous reasons this time she didn't look to her left. Breakfast!, she went to the kitchen in search of some soiled cup, some crust of bread. But everything was just as Clara herself had left it the night before, after washing the dinner dishes; Gladys never went out on her walks without making herself a cup of tea, and she always left everything on the table. The mother opened the front door and took a deep breath of the salty air. She firmly promised herself not to get frightened and to wait a while longer for her daughter to return. But what did those footsteps mean? weren't they a man's?

Exhausted she lay down on Gladys' unmade bed, thinking that all this was the girl's fault, because she never confided in her! What was there inside her daughter's heart?, she could only be sure of one thing, that Gladys always felt sad, "the rosemary nods upon the grave;/ the lily lolls upon the wave;/ wrapping the fog about its breast,/ The ruin moulders . . . at its best? . . . into a quest? . . . into a crest?" From the garden, through the gauze curtains, one could see Clara with her eyes wide open, staring at the ceiling; closer, behind the screen, her frequent sighs could also be heard, as if complaining about her bad memory. Distant thunder was heard, it came from the south, announcing a possible rainstorm, swept there by Antarctic winds: in a few minutes the coastal weather had changed for the worse.

Clara did not dare turn on the light, people said that light attracted lightning, and accustomed to the closeness of apartment buildings in Buenos Aires she felt at the mercy of the atmospheric electricity in that one-story house surrounded by small pine trees. In the dim light she rushed to check the closet and the bureau where Gladys kept her clothes, what had she put on to go out? Clara discovered that there were no street clothes missing. Suddenly her eyes fixed on the rack in the living room, where both she and Gladys hung their otter coats and . . . Clara's was missing! Then she went to the shoe boxes, no pair was missing. Her fine wool robe lay on a chair, her slippers were next to the bed and, her nightgown?, all search was useless, the nightgown had disappeared. Therefore Gladys had left the house barefoot, the furcoat over her nightgown.

But why her mother's old-fashioned furcoat? Clara did not doubt another moment, something very strange had happened. She put on street clothes and almost ran down the main street in the direction of the police station, with

8

the hope of getting there before it started raining, ". . . for her may some tall vault unfold—/ Some vault that oft hath flung its black/ And winged panels fluttering back,/ Some tomb from out whose sounding door/ She ne'er force an echo more,/ Thrilling to think, poor child of sin!/ It was the dead who . . . the dead who . . ."

And what was she going to say at the police station? Before anything she would warn them that this disappearance was not cause for alarm, that her daughter was an artist and consequently unpredictable in her reactions. She would add that Gladys was thirty-five years old, the truth, the winner of a prize for sculpture, and not in the province but in the city of Buenos Aires. Both mother and daughter had always lived in the big city, they were not small-town women. She would make it clear that Gladys was not very well known in Argentina, but a little in other countries. While she herself, as a poetess and a professional oral reader, was better known in her own country. She would add that it had nothing to do with differences in quality, in creative power, but it all came down to the fact that artists don't have the language barrier and poets unfortunately do. Clara turned around, suddenly she had the impression that someone was following her: a cream-colored car driven by a man wearing a hat was approaching her. But once beside her it didn't stop but continued its slow pace to the corner, disappearing when it turned. What else would she say at the police station?, it would be necessary to explain that Gladys was not a little girl who'd get lost if she let go of her mother's hand, no, she had lived alone for years outside the country. Any identification mark? Before, Gladys had never put on make-up, but with part of her face covered by a lock of hair—not by a bandage, nor by a pirate patch, only the frivolity of a lock—, the eye looked so beautiful when made up for the first time. . . . A young man had even said that that eye seemed like a humming-bird perched on her face, and what else could help the police?, she would ask the officer in charge of the case for discretion above all, and if her daughter soon reappeared

9

they should not let her know about the alarm, and of course they would have to hide from her the fact that an identification mark had been indicated.

It was true, Clara said to herself, with those imported false eyelashes the eye stands out more and looks radiantly beautiful, the blue eye with the green eyelid and the jet black lashes like the wings and erect tail of the humming-bird.

Reaching the corner where the cream-colored car had turned, Clara did the same and could make out a block away the black police van in front of the station house. And what if Gladys was already back home and it all turned out to be an embarrassing false alarm? The mother stopped, across the street was a small movie house, shut down by a municipal order. She hadn't passed by there for a while. The closing sign was stuck on the posters and covered the title of the last movie shown. Without a valid reason Clara walked over and read the police notice, perhaps hoping that it contained some sign of her daughter's whereabouts, a sign of providence. The notice only said that the hall was being closed for reasons of public hygiene and safety.

There were also other governmental proclamations stuck to the façade which pressed for law and order and recommended the capture of activists listed there; Clara did not read them. Suddenly she had reached the conclusion that her daughter was already on her way home, because Gladys too was frightened by storms. Clara began to retrace her steps. Besides if the patrolmen searched for Gladys and found her on a road in a nightgown and a fur-coat, they would consider her a lunatic and submit her to treatment intolerable to the girl's sensitivity, "may her sleep,/ which is enduring, so be deep!/ Heaven have her in its sacred keep!/ This chamber changed for one more holy,/ This bed for one more . . . more . . ." what came next? she looked at her wristwatch, it was nine-thirty A.M., what wouldn't she have given to know where her daughter was at that very moment! "may her sleep,/ which is so

10

enduring, so be deep!/ Heaven have her in its sacred keep!/ This chamber changed for one more holy,/ This bed for one . . . for one . . . for one . . . more melancholy!! I pray to God that she may lie/ Forever with unopened eye,/ While the dim sheeted ghosts go by!," finally she remembered, to her satisfaction.

II

Veronica Lake: (a bad-tempered girl, with half of her beautiful face hidden by long silky blond hair, drives a car; a strange impulse makes her stop at the sight of a man in the rain) Get in.

The stranger: (he gets in and turns out to be very handsome, his expression inscrutable) Why did you stop?

Veronica Lake: I saw you in the rain . . . (silence) I never give a ride to strangers, I don't know why I stopped for you. (silence follows again, she'd like him to ask more questions, he doesn't; she feels that a match has started and that she's lost her first round already)

(from *The Blue Dahlia*, Paramount Pictures)

Buenos Aires, May 21, 1969

He stands in the middle of the room, his body alert. His only garment is a towel, wrapped around his waist, which doesn't cover the tensed muscles of his hairy calves, while his strong arms, thrust forward, display contracted hands with arched fingers. His half-opened mouth shows surprise. His ear is turned toward the front door: the starting of a car engine in second gear, eight stories below, mixes with, but doesn't cover, the squeak of a metal elevator door opening onto that same floor of the apartment building. The water dripping from a faucet in the kitchen produces, on the other hand, an imperceptible sound. Also imperceptible are the vibration of the filament of a lighted bulb in the bathroom that's about to blow out, and the passage of hot steam through the heating system composed of two visible radiators and pipes hidden inside the wall. His bare feet are stepping on a natural-colored checkered jute rug. The braided jute rug, slightly rough to the touch, partially covers the waxed and consequently slippery wooden floor. But the most polished surface belongs to a French crystal ashtray. Also smooth to the touch are a ceramic jug hand-painted in enamel, the mixed fabric of silk and synthetic fibre covering two chairs, the tiles and sanitary implements in the bathroom, the hairless sectors of his skin— back, shoulders, buttocks, part of the chest—and almost all of the skin of the woman lying still on the bed. The roughest surface belongs to a painting by a contemporary artist from the "tachiste" school, whose clots of paint result in granular and even pointy reliefs; its predominant colors are yellow and black. There are several other paintings in the apartment, among them one of unusual dimensions— two yards high and one yard wide—almost totally filled by an indigo blue circle on a grey background. Against one of the walls—all of them painted white—there's a single bed, the blue sheets have a dark blue border and the two blankets are light brown. The woman's skin is very white, the gag in her mouth has been improvised out of a man's silk handkerchief, multi-colored but sober, her hands fastened behind her with a mourning tie. The color of the woman's eyes cannot be seen because they are closed, besides, under her left eyelid the corresponding eyeball is missing. On the rest of the body there are no signs of violence, such as purple bruises or wounds clotted with dark blood. Neither is there any sign of sexual violence. The six cigarette butts divided between the crystal ashtray and another bronze one show no traces of lipstick. The wrought bronze ashtray from India contains the only lighted cigarette, the

13

smoke draws a straight vertical line. A slight smell of burnt tobacco comes from both ashtrays, noticeable only a few inches away. Also a few inches from the surface it emanates from it is possible to scent—near the woman's neck—a sweet French perfume and—near his armpits— the characteristic acid smell of perspiration. This perspiration has also dampened the armpits of a shirt—the two stains produced are oval—, now hanging on a chair with other male garments. There are also dampness stains on the ceiling, in various tones of green, and under the bathroom sink the cracked layer of plaster and paint is also shaded by the dust sticking there, not wiped away during cleaning procedures to avoid the possibility of enlarging the cracks. A few inches lower, on the floor next to the washstand base, lies a piece of absorbent cotton soaked in chloroform, now partially evaporated. In the kitchen too there's a piece of cotton, next to a red injection vial; on the same marble surface there's another vial, but broken and empty, whose sides are tinted by the yellowish liquid they once contained. A few inches away, on the stove, one can see a rectangular metal container with water to sterilize the syringe and its corresponding hypodermic needle. The only window in the kitchen is decorated with a curtain, made of a very light linen material which is raised by the passage of a slight breeze. That same breeze, on the other hand, is not strong enough to modify the position of the remaining objects in the kitchen, including the piece of cotton since it's weighted down with alcohol. Hanging on the wall opposite the stove are several utensils and also decorative details among which a bronze and wooden electric clock that says 9:30, stands out. Also bronze are the handles on the cupboard drawers. The silverware, can openers, and corkscrews are kept in the highest drawer. But the sharpest edge belongs to the kitchen-knife, usually kept, because of its large size, in the more spacious second drawer next to the everyday napkins and tablecloths. It is not there at this moment, and besides it would be hard to determine whether or not that knife is sharper than the rustproof steel scissors brought as a gift from Toledo, and placed on the desk in the main room beside a pile of magazines and newspapers with articles marked for clipping, a few inches from an almost blunt-edged paper cutter. The above-mentioned scissors have received special chemical treatment giving them a golden shine and they're among the glossiest objects in the room, together with the silver-plated ring on the standing lamp, the mother-of-pearl polished nails of the reclining woman and the crystal ashtray. On the other hand the knife's blade cannot reflect and refract rays of light because it is covered by the mattress on the only bed in the apartment. Besides, the metal is poorly polished because of the inefficient cleaning method and seems rusty in parts, especially near the jagged edges. In the light, however, one could appraise that knife as an unusual kitchen tool, since it is a costly piece from Morocco, abundant in details of subtle craftsmanship. Also expensive are the paintings, all by famous artists, a hi-fidelity record player and a Smith 38 revolver, loaded with six bullets and kept in one of the drawers in the night table. The least valuable object in the room is a nearly empty match box. Besides, this object is one of the lightest in the room, together with the loose pages lying on the desk, an ostrich feather pen in an old-fashioned inkwell, a synthetic nightgown thrown in a corner, and a pair of long-fine metal needles. The latter are instruments used in acu-puncture, the age old Chinese medical science whose practitioners detect right on the skin the invisible points which have to be punctured, for diverse purposes: vital energy circulates on the surface of the skin without ever stopping, fulfilling as an index of equilibrium a symmetrical course, until death, and that equilibrium can be preserved—or broken—according to the will of those practitioners, since they have only to stick the long needle—it doesn't leave traces—in some specific point. The aforementioned squeak of the metal elevator door corresponds to the action executed by a woman at the moment of closing it. That woman has one hand on the doorknob and the other on her purse, which she clings to nervously. The position of her body shows that she will go toward the door of the apartment where the man in the towel is listening, with an expression of inordinate excitement, to the sounds approaching from the hallway.

III

Joan Crawford: (a very rich New Yorker, tired of everything except her new lover, who's turned out to be as elusive as she likes the idea of happiness to be) Is Philadelphia the end of the world? Why didn't you call me, why didn't you write?

The young virtuoso: Those rehearsals were endless, I was too busy, I had other things to do

Joan Crawford: (finally losing all self-respect) Paul, what good is a woman when she can't be good to anyone?

(from *Humoresque*, Warner Bros.)

PRINCIPAL EVENTS IN GLADYS' LIFE

Gladys Hebe D'Onofrio was born in Buenos Aires on January 2, 1935, the daughter of Clara Evelia Llanos and Pedro Alejandro D'Onofrio. She was conceived on the morning of Sunday, May 29, 1934, after her parents returned from a performance of Eugene O'Neill's "The Great God Brown" in the Teatro del Universo, Buenos Aires, followed by a public debate. During the performance, Clara Evelia Llanos de D'Onofrio felt that her poetic vocation was coming back to life, spurred on by the avant-garde nature of the play. She decided to resume her writing the next day if the weather was good and her husband could proceed with the plan to go fishing, which one of his colleagues at the 4th Branch of the Banco Industrial Argentino had proposed. During the first months of married life Clara Evelia had been engrossed by her new tasks as housewife and had not felt the need to write. The edition of her only book of poems published to date, titled "Greening" and signed with a pseudonym, Clara Ariel, had been financed out of her savings. But she had not yet achieved her main goal: to be included—at least two titles, "There Were Sea Grapes" and "How Melancholy Are Brides"—in the repertoire of Berta Singerman, the most important oral reader in the country. Pedro Alejandro D'Onofrio also reacted favorably to the play, partly because he already knew two other works by the playwright, both in screen adaptations. That fact allowed him to converse freely with his wife, who generally knew more works than he did, and during the debate he even felt the desire to participate, but he was afraid he didn't have the proper vocabulary: if his wife hadn't been present he would have ventured to express some opinion. Clara Evelia also did not give her opinion because in some way she feared, praising that play which had really impressed her, a betrayal of her own esthetic principles. She felt said principles to be virtually embraced by two words: grace and refinement.

Back home Clara Evelia expressed the desire to reread her masters, Nervo and Darío; her husband would have preferred to put out the light the minute they got into bed because it was already two-thirty in the morning, but he had promised himself never to antagonize his wife in situations related to poetry. Clara Evelia put out the light almost an hour later, Pedro Alejandro was sleeping. Clara Evelia got up silently and looked at the sky which was lit in the distance by faint lightning. She would not follow up her plan to write the next day if the weather was bad. She went back to bed and could not avoid thinking of two consecrated names which humiliated her: the poetesses Juana de Ibarbarou and Alfonsina Storni. Clara Evelia had a bitter taste in her mouth, she imagined herself green and

18

with black rings under her eyes, the embodiment of envy. A little later she heard the sound of raindrops. She looked at her husband sleeping on his side with his back to her, she moved close to him and looked for an unusual place to kiss him: she considered his earlobe, a mole on his back, and a protuberance on his shoulderblade. She wanted to give a kiss full of grace and refinement. She decided on the earlobe and kissed it without getting a response. She bit it gently. Pedro Alejandro woke up and the sex act over, returning from the bathroom he asked his wife to repeat something nice that she had read that night. She repeated the first thing she remembered: ". . . there was a beautiful garden nearby, with more roses than azaleas and more violets than roses." He exclaimed "how nice" and closed his eyes to go back to sleep; she again felt sour saliva thickening in her throat, she would have preferred the request to favor a poem of her own making.

During her pregnancy Clara Evelia bore in mind her doctor's advice and spent long hours of repose listening on the radio to relaxing music when she could find it—broadcast by the national stations—, otherwise she'd resort to her record player and forcibly repeat her limited repertory: Handel's "Largo," Sibelius' "Swan of Tuonela" and "Valse Triste," Moussorgsky's "Pictures at an Exhibition," Beethoven's "Ninth Symphony," and the almost complete piano works of Albéniz. A few days after the end of her seventh month, her brother-in-law José Luis D'Onofrio lost his life together with his wife, María Esther, in a car accident: Clara Evelia went to the wake insisting upon staying beside her husband the whole night. At dawn she felt sick and a few days later gave birth to a baby girl weighing only five pounds.

Gladys was nursed until fourteen months old by her mother who at that time felt her crises of literary frustration recurring. When someone would ask her what she wanted her daughter to be when she grew up, she'd immediately remember that this kind of question had been put to her twenty years back and she had answered "I want to be a ballerina" or "I want to be a dramatic actress." Clara

Evelia would look at her baby and think that now there was not only one but two souls thirsting for fame and recognition.

The maternal grandmother, two paternal aunts and the next door neighbor in the house where they moved soon after Gladys' birth, in the Villa Devoto district, took turns in the care of the child. The neighbor especially took charge of the little girl when Clara Evelia attended lectures and matinée theater performances, alone, since she had lost contact with her old friends. This drifting apart had begun with the publication of her book; her acquaintances had let her down by asking her for a free copy, instead of helping her to recover the cost of the edition by buying it; besides she interpreted their reticence to comment on the book as an unmistakable sign of envy.

During a performance of Lope de Vega's *The Foolish Lady*, Clara Evelia ran into an old classmate from the conservatory where both had studied elocution and piano. Her friend introduced her to two young girls as her advanced students in elocution. During an aside she explained to her that, overwhelmed with work, that afternoon she had preferred to pay for her pupils' family circle tickets instead of giving them a class, with the pretext that they needed to become acquainted with the Spanish classical theater. She even offered Clara a student whom she had rejected the day before because of the lack of available time.

Clara Evelia accepted and a few months later had eight students whom she'd teach only in the morning and with whose payments she could balance the new budget which included a maid and the project to publish a second book of poetry.

Mother and daughter

Gladys Hebe was partial to the above-mentioned neighbor, who had afforded her the unforgettable emotion of a Sunday trip to the Paraná Delta, and in this neighbor's house she would eat everything that was put on her plate

20

and would take her nap without protest, which didn't happen in her own home. Her aunts and grandmother were jealous and felt glad when the neighbor had to move with her husband, a Customs supervisor, to his new appointment in Paso de los Libres. Gladys Hebe was then four years old and when her mother scolded her for not eating, she'd cry recalling silently that during the excursion to the Delta she had eaten while sitting on the neighbor's lap, which on the other hand was due to the fact that they had not bought her a ticket of her own, making her pass for a baby. Gladys Hebe called to the neighbor in her dreams only, because otherwise her mother would give her bitter looks.

At age five she was sent to the "Tom Thumb" private kindergarten. The teacher taught her a poem and the child learned it more rapidly than her classmates. Clara Evelia didn't find out about this until the teacher congratulated her one day when the maid couldn't pick the child up after school. Clara Evelia was surprised because the child had always refused to learn even the shortest poems from her. Once back at the house the mother asked her daughter to recite it. Gladys resisted, her mother threatened to write to their former neighbor and to tell her not to come back to Buenos Aires anymore because the child had died. The child recited, Clara Evelia said that the teacher was a "donkey" and that she had taught her "donkey's" gestures. The child looked at her defiantly and said that the teacher recited better than Clara Evelia because she was prettier. For the first time she thought of comparing the teacher's thin, pale pink hands with filed but short unpolished nails, to her mother's hands, with dark olive tobacco-stained fingers and long arched nails painted vermilion red. Clara Evelia cried. The child saw her mother cry for the first time and could never forget the drops, black with mascara, which rolled down her cheeks.

The next year Gladys entered first grade in the "Paula Albarracín de Sarmiento" public school, in spite of being a year under the required age. From then until sixth grade she was the best student in her class. Her mother tried only once, when Gladys was not yet seven, to make her participate in the end term recitals which she performed with her pupils. It was a long dramatized poem, about a noble lady who with her daughter embroidered the first Argentine flag. Clara's goal was to show that little children could memorize and consequently take elocution lessons. The recital took place in the "Taricco" movie theater on San Martín Avenue, rented especially for a Wednesday at 6:00 P.M. The first part went smoothly, the participating children skillfully passed over the minor slips of memory. When the curtain was raised for the second part to begin, mother and daughter were on the stage, seated in their respective chairs with a tablecloth between them substituting for the flag. The daughter began the dialogue with a voice strangled with fear, the mother continued with consummate professionalism. The daughter continued her part, praising the stitches her mother made on the national cloth with skillful hands. While the mother recited the next reply, Gladys, as if someone were whispering in her ear, heard a question, "Could the character represented by your mother embroider well in spite of having dark hands and nails like a bird of prey?" Suddenly there was an unexpected silence in the hall: Gladys had forgotten her lines. Her mother took charge of the child's reply and continued with her own: a new silence, Gladys could not remember her part. From then on Clara Evelia recited the text of both characters. As soon as the curtain fell, Gladys ran to the toilet backstage and locked herself in. The other participants carried on perfectly and when her turn came Clara Evelia, overexcited by the incident, acted with more zeal than usual and found new tones for certain painful passages of the Chilean authoress Gabriela Mistral, whose poem "Sterility" closed the program.

Father and daughter

Gladys' aptitude for drawing was revealed from the time of her early schooling. She'd go to class in the morning and in the afternoon she'd quickly do her homework so that by four o'clock she'd be free to listen with the maid to the soap opera on Radio Belgrano. They'd sit in the kitchen and from four-thirty until dinner time Gladys would copy in a notebook the drawings from the Chicks section in "Wise Guy," the funnies magazine that her father bought every Thursday. Gladys thought that her father—who so much liked the kind of girl that was a "dish," according to his own expression—would be happy if she grew up to be like a girl from "Wise Guy." They were invariably very tall with tans, narrow waists, floating round bosoms, and long fleshy legs. The face was always small, with a very turned-up nose, long straight hair with curled-up tips, and a big lock of hair almost covering one of the large, green, almond-shaped eyes which occupied most of the face. Gladys was always anxious for Thursday to come so that she could make new copies of the page dedicated to Chicks, she'd feel a tremendous joy at beginning each meticulous copy though toward the middle of each work she'd feel somewhat ashamed for always drawing the same subject.

But the notebooks continued to be filled with the same girl in different positions, until one day she decided to draw only faces which would occupy the whole page, as suggested by a new friend, her benchmate in High School 3, which she had just entered that March 1947. Her benchmate's name was Fanny Zuckelmann and she had reacted with a look of scorn when Gladys showed her the copies from "Wise Guy." The next day Fanny brought to class the drawing book belonging to her older sister, an advanced student in a private school of fine arts. Gladys felt humiliated and not knowing how to do better she began to draw a series of faces of actresses, sure of achieving a better result than that obtained by Fanny's sister in a portrait of the movie actress Ingrid Bergman executed in color pencil. Firstly Gladys drew Vivien Leigh, although she wasn't one of her favorites, because she considered her the only actress with as much prestige as Ingrid Bergman. But she couldn't get the likeness right and all her attempts were frustrated: it was difficult to recognize the model.

She hid it all from Fanny, which did not prevent a new clash with her classmate before the end of the first month of school. Fanny asked her what book she was reading, Gladys answered that at night she listened to the radio in the kitchen until her parents took the appliance into their bedroom to listen to the news. Fanny asked her if she knew of Hermann Hesse, Thomas Mann and Lion Feuchtwanger. Gladys was hearing their names for the first time and tried not to make it noticeable. Covered by Fanny so that it looked like a textbook, Hermann Hesse's *Demian* impressed Gladys so much that she couldn't sleep at night and during those hours of insomnia she reached the conclusion that she was not the only one unlucky for no reason at all, Demian was too. They had always told her that she should be grateful for being born in a home like hers, where she had everything: food, a roof, clothes and studies, while other children her age had nothing. After *Demian* came a long series of contemporary European novels which allowed Gladys to identify with numerous characters affected by the *mal du siècle:* the anguish of existence as she was told by Fanny, who had listened to conversations on this subject at the home of her cousin, a violinist in the Municipal Symphonic Orchestra.

One morning Gladys came to class looking down, Fanny nudged her with her elbow because she hadn't greeted her and when Gladys said "hello" she showed her front teeth covered with braces. She had to wear them four years, until after the Sweet Fifteen Dance; she needed to unburden herself and with tears in her eyes she ventured a confession, she told Fanny that with each day her anguish of existence grew worse. Fanny, as if deprived of her own vocabulary and ideas, reacted scornfully: she said that according to psychoanalysis anguish didn't come from being but from not being what we wanted, "you're anguished because you don't have straight teeth like mine," and she showed her a homogeneous row of short, yellowish teeth. Gladys saw that they were short and yellowish but she didn't have the courage to return the insult, she remained silent.

The next Saturday Fanny celebrated her birthday with a hot chocolate party and family and friends came to her house; Gladys was the only classmate invited. At the party she finally met Fanny's older sister, Buby, sixteen years old, a fat and rather awkward girl. Gladys asked Buby to show her all her drawings and engraved in her memory the address of the school, written with little Roman letters on the front sheet of each notebook. Whenever Fanny had spoken to her in class about that sister who studied fine arts, Gladys had imagined her beautiful and artistic, meaning by artistic a sensitive, dreamy girl, always in harmonious poses, barefoot and half-covered by veils. Gladys had never conceived of the possibility of attending a school of fine arts because she didn't feel capable of filling those personal requirements. The following Monday during class Fanny told her that her family had found Gladys too shy for her age, and during recreation, while Fanny hurriedly studied a lesson, Gladys truthfully told the other girls that Fanny's apartment looked very small, which was why her big sister had to sleep in the living room and Fanny in the same room as her parents.

The following Thursday Pedro Alejandro D'Onofrio got back from work with the new issue of "Wise Guy," as usual. Gladys took it out of his hand and looked at the Chicks section, the whole page was occupied by one cartoon: two elegant and Donjuanesque-looking friends were about to turn a corner where two girls with whom they had a date were waiting for them, one attractive and the other deformed and bearded. One of the young men was saying to the other that his beautiful girlfriend had promised to bring another friend no less beautiful. Gladys' father laughed again upon remembering the joke and said: "the poor guy is stuck with the dog." When someone alluded to an ugly woman with that expression Gladys felt implicated, something which also happened to her with

25

the word spinster. When anyone said those words Gladys looked in the other direction. At that moment her mother appeared and tore the magazine out of the girl's hand, "enough bending over this garbage the whole day long!" she cried out, and she complained to her husband that Gladys spent the day with her head bent over, her shoulders rounded, and her chest sunk in, "in spite of all my suggestions she didn't want to sign up for the basketball team and look how she is, skinny and yellow, and now she wants to sign up for art school to make herself even more bent over." Next Gladys heard what she had always been afraid of hearing from her father's lips, but she heard the sentence before it was said, as if someone had whispered it in her ear. It all happened in a few seconds, her father seemed to read the sentence telepathically in his daughter's thoughts and he articulated aloud the feared words: "You have to pay attention to Mommy, because Daddy doesn't want to have a dog for a daughter."

Vocation

The "Leonardo da Vinci" Institute was open from three in the afternoon until twelve at night. Gladys signed up for drawing classes twice a week and in the middle of the year she signed up for sculpture as well. To compensate for those hours she'd spend over the easel or clay her parents decided to make her a member of a sports club, where she'd go Saturdays and Sundays accompanied by her mother. Her father didn't sign up because he preferred to devote those days to fishing. Clara Evelia made use of a wealthy student in order to be recommended for the Barrancas Club, which was exclusive and therefore difficult to get into. Gladys on the other hand wanted to go to the same club as Fanny, one of the largest in the city, but Clara Evelia didn't want to because according to her it was full of Jews. During the first month mother and daughter went every Saturday and Sunday: they would go after lunch, they would visit all the sections and one by one

26

their attempts to integrate into groups were frustrated. Clara Evelia decided to buy a tennis racquet and outfit for Gladys the following month, in order to sign her up for the classes they offered on Saturdays. Meanwhile she patiently waited for the wealthy student to appear one day with her family. It was the only chance of being introduced to other members.

The meeting took place on the fifth weekend of consecutive attendance and for the first time mother and daughter had their tea with company. The following Saturday the student did not attend the club and neither did her family. Clara Evelia and daughter passed by the table of a group to which the student had introduced them but they weren't invited to sit down. They sat at one of the small tables and ordered tea and toast. The following month went by and the purchase of the tennis equipment did not materialize.

During the cold months it rained several times on the weekends and Clara decided that they wouldn't return to the club until summer, since by then the swimming pool would be open and they wouldn't need company to spend a pleasant moment there.

Gladys' progress at the school of fine arts was, on the other hand, rapid and indisputable. Her clay models in particular attracted attention. Her nocturnal readings were considerably reduced and Fanny's upsetting remarks found her less vulnerable. The summer having arrived she did not wish to discontinue her classes but at the same time she registered for the swimming lessons at the club, which were administered to groups selected according to height, where surprisingly she made friends with other girls in her group: she was often invited to large tables where the younger people had cold drinks. Her mother preferred to stay home. Years later Gladys would remember that period—the summer of 1948—as the happiest time of her life.

At the end of March her menstrual periods, painful and irregular, began. In April the "Leonardo da Vinci" Insti-

27

tute started the academic year and from the first class Gladys could not take her eyes off a new drawing student. The young man was eighteen, wore his hair unusually long with virile impertinence and had regular, sensitive features. Most outstanding were his blue and slanty eyes. Gladys took pains in her work to attract the young man's attention, but she did not succeed until they also coincided in their sculpture classes. There she could not pass unobserved because the teacher's praise fell too often upon her. At the end of the year the teacher decided to present works for the upcoming Fall Art Show. The young man contributed a gigantic Icarus and Gladys a life-sized head of a child. Gladys wanted the young man to win the prize and also wanted to win it herself in order to arouse his admiration. When she saw the works exhibited in the hall she thought that hers would pass unnoticed and concentrated all her expectations on the awarding of the Icarus. She let the young man know this. He invited her to a cold drink at a bar and Gladys was almost certain that with the years she would gain the young man's love.

The prize was awarded in March 1949 and Gladys came out the youngest winner in the history of the prize: fourteen years old. Gladys was embraced by her mother. Clara cried and her tears ran black with mascara. Gladys looked among the crowd for other eyes, blue, slanty and without make-up. She found them, but the young man looked at her briefly without greeting her and, disdainful, he turned his face in the other direction.

First parties

The first high school classmate to be fifteen gave a party at her house and Gladys was invited, but the boys present considered her too young to be asked to dance. Nevertheless she had a pleasant time talking to the birthday girl's older brother and his girlfriend. The subject of conversation were the novels *Point Counterpoint* by Aldous Huxley and Thomas Mann's *The Transposed Heads*. When the couple left, Gladys remained alone sitting in her chair and had to wait in that position for an hour until her father came to get her.

During that school year and the following Gladys saw the number of young admirers, waiting for her classmates after school, multiply. She had the impression that they were spontaneously generated, they would appear one day on the sidewalk where the day before there had been nothing, like mushrooms or weeds. Gladys maintained the appearance of a little school girl and, in fact, she was one or two years younger than her classmates, besides having been prematurely born.

Sexually there were three important episodes during her prolonged adolescence. The first took place at the "Leonardo da Vinci" Institute, when a male model substituted for the usual female model of the year before. The day of the first session, Gladys had come to class full of excited curiosity, took her usual place and was preparing the work materials when the boy entered the classroom and began to undress. Gladys lowered her eyes, the wooden floor made of boards looked dry and colorless but recently swept. The boy was short and stocky but athletic-looking, with strong muscles and a sex organ of unusual dimensions. Gladys looked at the model, now up on his platform and taking the position which the teacher indicated. The teacher had told the students beforehand about the boy's inexperience and desperate need for work, with his wife in the hospital and an infant son. Gladys had believed until then that all men had a small penis like the Greek statues. The terror and excitement shook her deeply, her glands started activating at a new speed. She thought of the terrible pain that being possessed by a man would entail.

The second sexual event took place the following year, right after a conversation with Fanny. The latter was now sixteen years old and one day during chemistry class she began to cry when the teacher gave her a zero for not knowing the lesson. Gladys was surprised because Fanny

29

didn't care about grades and during recreation she asked her what was the matter. Fanny told her that at home they were opposed to her courtship with a young Catholic and that she couldn't leave him because every Saturday evening that year she had surrendered to him after the movies. Gladys felt that the school's tile courtyard was made of floor boards as in the classroom at the "Leonardo da Vinci" Institute, and that it was starting to slant, until the boards disappeared under her feet and both fell into a black abyss: Gladys imagined the deep wound in Fanny's flesh, the only thing visible was the wound, white and pink like bacon, in that black abyss where one could hear but not see a river running which could be red like blood. When Gladys in turn was sixteen she concluded that her virginity as well was in danger because Fanny had lost it at that age, and she was afraid to go home alone, because of the dark streets that she had to pass on her way back from the Institute.

But before then, the third event occurred: a classmate from the Institute suggested that they go on a double date with the girl's suitor and a friend of his. Gladys happily accepted because that classmate deserved her confidence. The young man's appearance reassured her completely, he was thin and weak like her. They stopped at a tea shop downtown and afterwards they went for a walk in the Retiro Park. Gladys suggested sitting in the lighted section where there were stone benches. Her friend in turn suggested that Gladys stay there with her companion while she went with hers toward the isolated area near the port. Gladys neither wished to remain alone with her suitor nor abandon her friend: she preferred to run the risk of going into the dark area. Her friend was walking several steps ahead, suddenly she stopped and, smiling, she asked them to increase the distance that separated one couple from the other. Gladys' companion took her hand, she did not withdraw it. They walked a few yards more in the opposite direction until Gladys stopped, so as not to get too far from

30

her friend. The young man kissed her by surprise. Gladys kept her mouth shut and looked in the direction of the other couple. Gladys felt that the young man's member was erect, unpleasant nervous discharges shook her body and she broke loose. A half hour of arguments followed, after which they reached the agreement that Gladys would let herself be kissed if the boy didn't hug her. During all that time Gladys watched her friend from afar, to her relief the rim of the girl's skirt never rose, though the two pressed together and seemed like a single shadow outlined against the lamppost. As far as her suitor's advances were concerned, Gladys did not have to worry about them in the future, because he never again asked her for a date.

By mutual agreement with her parents

By mutual agreement with her parents, after finishing high school, Gladys went on to a state university of fine arts to continue her study of sculpture. At the same time she registered at an academy to learn English and decided to take on private drawing students. This way she was busy the whole day. In the new school she soon became friends with another student, Alicia Bonelli, thirty-one years of age. Alicia was a primary school teacher and had decided to resume her studies despite her apprehension about having classmates younger than herself.

The four years that followed were serene ones for Gladys. The problem of idle time on Saturday and Sunday, which had pressured her because she didn't have anyone to go out with, was solved because she would go to the movies or theater with Alicia, even when it was pouring rain. Subjects of conversation were never lacking because both were fascinated by the various art forms. When Alicia thought it appropriate she told Gladys, with discretion and modesty, the story of her relationship with a married man whom she had just stopped seeing a few months ago, upon deciding to go back to her studies.

31

Political awareness

On September 26, 1955, a revolution overthrew the regime of Juan Domingo Perón. Gladys had not gone to class for fear of street riots, she got up late and asked the maid—working in her mother's house for just a few months, lately the hired help didn't last since Clara would ration the food—to make her some coffee. The maid served her a cup and unable to hold back the tears any longer went running to her room. Gladys sympathized with the girl and went to tell her—not knowing what else to do—that the new government would not abandon the working class, on the contrary, it would bring progress and well-being to the country. The girl continued to cry without answering. Gladys asked herself why she was so happy about the fall of Perón: because it was a Fascist regime, she answered, and it was necessary to remember what Hitler and Mussolini had been capable of doing in power. Gladys was also happy because without Perón there would be no further risk of their suspending the importation of foreign fashion magazines and movies, and her mother wouldn't have any more problems with the hired help. And the inflation would stop.

Professional preparation

As far as her professional preparation was concerned, Gladys continued making technical progress, but a pronounced tendency to respect the traditional rules, and even an unconscious complacency in copying established artists, were undermining her possibilities of personal expression. According to her adversaries, this was the main reason why in 1959 she was awarded the annual scholarship for pursuing advanced studies in the United States for fifteen months. Gladys was then twenty-four. The application for the scholarship had been her main reason for living during the two years following her graduation and she was sure that if she won it all her problems would be solved: in the United States, as a foreigner, her personality would become mysterious and attractive, and at some mundane reception she would meet an impetuous conductor of some symphonic orchestra, either Hungarian or Austrian, and possibly an English novelist, thus unleashing an inevitable love triangle. Her imagination always preferred European personalities, usually exiles from some tragic conflict like the Second World War.

Alicia Bonelli had never sympathized with the USA but she had refrained from making adverse comments on the trip until it became definite. Then she did disapprove of the project and told Gladys that the USA was the octopus that strangled Latin America, and she considered it treason to study there. Gladys replied that that country was the cradle of democracy. Alicia replied that if she were black she wouldn't think so. Gladys did not wish to continue the argument and wondered to herself how Alicia could sympathize with the USSR, having such evidence against it like the books *Out of the Night* by Jan Valtin and *I Choose Freedom* by Victor Kravchenko, besides the movie *The Iron Curtain* with Gene Tierney and Dana Andrews.

Overseas

Upon her arrival, Washington was covered with snow. The city was the perfect setting for the dreams she had conceived. The house where she lodged was a pretty two-story cottage, her room faced the small backyard where the owners' grandchildren played, when they came to visit on Sundays. The rest of the week Mr. and Mrs. Ellison received few visitors and the silence of the house was barely upset by a distant sound of voices which came from the television set. Gladys did not introduce any change in the decoration of her room because she liked the impersonal character of that furniture typical of inexpensive hotels of the thirties: smooth surfaces and spare ornaments. Gladys was also pleased with the affectionate but distant treatment she received from the old couple and she never had to give them any explanations if some Saturday or Sunday afternoon she remained alone in her room.

Gladys could not become interested in the theory classes at the Virginia Center for the Arts and neither did she decide to spend the money necessary to acquire the work implements. The excitement she got from her visits to museums—where she had free access—fulfilled her daily aspirations of renewal. Her plan matured very rapidly: she would apply for a resident's visa to remain in the country once the course was over, and she would look for work. Because of that she reduced her budget to a minimum and avoided going out with friends of the opposite sex since they always shared the expenses; they liked places of alcoholic consumption, a dispensable luxury. Gladys thought that it would take her some time to find a job.

Adaptation to the environment

In her Art History class she made friends with a fifty-year-old woman auditing the class, who reminded her a lot of Alicia. Alicia's letters arrived every Thursday and Gladys answered them punctually. Mary Ann Schonn was the student's name, and Gladys soon found herself repeating by letter to Alicia the same words she'd say to Mary Ann, either in class or at the apartment occupied by her new friend and her husband, Ralph. They were a childless couple, Ralph worked from nine to five in the publicity department of an important company and Mary Ann took care of the house and worked on her ceramics, suggested by the psychoanalyst who had taken care of her when Mary Ann had to leave her job because of a nervous breakdown. Ralph did not oppose any of his wife's decisions, afraid of a possible hysterical outburst, and happily welcomed Gladys' appearance on the scene, because his wife would talk at length to her leaving him free to read the newspaper, to solve the crossword puzzle, and to look at the action serials on TV. Her scholarship over, Gladys obtained with the help of Mary Ann's patronage the residence permit she so much desired. That patronage consisted of a letter from Gladys' American friend in which she vouchsafed the girl's honesty and accepted responsibility for her conduct.

Residence in the USA

Gladys quickly got a job as a secretary in Spanish for an export-import company, where she worked eight hours a day. Her vague plans for renting a loft and resuming her sculpture were indefinitely postponed. First of all she wanted to save the thousand-dollar security necessary for remaining in the country without patronage, since it bothered her to owe that favor to the Schonns. Once she had that sum in her savings account, her next project was to travel to California with Mary Ann, when she had a vacation. This desire fulfilled, she planned to renew her wardrobe, to buy a television set, and to start her own collection of art books.

Thus passed three years, during which time she had the opportunity of seeing again, on television, all her favorite movies—*Humoresque, Camille, I'll Cry Tomorrow, The Blue Dahlia, Tender Comrade, Marie Antoinette*, etc.— and also to change jobs as a bilingual secretary several times, always with a raise in salary, until she decided to stay at one company for special reasons: the son of one of the owners would come to the office twice a week, serving as a link with the office in New York where he lived. Gladys awaited those appearances with the same excitement she had experienced before at the threshold of Washington's museums.

The young Robert Giusto had points in common with the three ideal prototypes of North American male that Gladys had conceived miles away in her distant Argentina, but which were secondbest to her European models. Those three prefigurations were the following: a) the hypersensitive and tenderly neurotic young heir with the face of the young Montgomery Clift; b) the married man, a successful entrepreneur, feverishly active, dominating but in need of understanding in his inner self, with the face of John Kennedy; c) the young, athletic, inexperienced-looking college man, full of faith in the future, with the face of the blond baseball players who recommended various commercial products in the magazines. Robert, called Bob by everybody, was tall, athletic, tanned, polite, and slightly shy, with regular features and an innocent expression, therefore a summary of the aforementioned types. But he was soon to marry a young woman with money, and during that premarital period Gladys made the effort of accepting dates from two young men. But they contrasted physically with the girl's favorite prototypes, besides having a fault unpardonable in Gladys' eyes: a lack of conversation. For example, the fact that they didn't know her favorite novelists (Mann, Hesse, and Huxley) convinced her that the young men had nothing to talk about.

Returning from a concert she had attended with Mary Ann, the night of Saturday the 27th, September 1962, Gladys found a telegram under her door. When she arrived in Buenos Aires her father had already passed away; listening to her mother's pleas she telephoned her boss and asked for a leave which was granted. During that two-week stay in Buenos Aires, Gladys found out that some of her ex-classmates had already given exhibitions in important galleries and that one of them was developing a distinguished career in Paris. Few hadn't married. She found it all out through Alicia, whom she had stopped writing to some time ago. The above-named appeared with a Bohemian-looking woman friend, and to Gladys' astonishment, when her mother left the room, the two women embraced and informed her that they were very happy together. In the following meeting Alicia confessed to her ex-classmate that women had always interested her sexually and that the long love story with a married man had been real except that instead of a man it had been a woman.

As far as the subject of politics was concerned, Gladys

avoided it but Alicia brought it up as much as she could: she reprimanded the USA for the Cuba blockade, "see how they are, as soon as a Latin American country wants to govern itself they try to strangle it." Gladys replied that Cuba was horrible because there were shortages of all kinds. The argument did not continue for long because Gladys went on to talk about the problem of her mother's widowhood.

Hard times

Back in Washington Gladys had difficulties in returning to her customary rhythm of life. She was especially bothered by the insomnia she brought back with her from Buenos Aires and she refrained from taking tranquilizers for fear of creating a habit. The only stimulating news was the temporary separation between Bob and his wife.

On November 29, 1962, she was upset at the office because of a mistake she made, absent-mindedly, which would cost the company an embarrassing delay with a customer, and walking back home she saw the first Christmas show windows of the season: the most important family holiday was approaching. A sudden fit of hysterical weeping shook her and she couldn't hold it back, she took a side street and walked several blocks to unburden herself. She decided not to go to Mary Ann's house as she had planned because Mary Ann would notice that she was troubled and would again advise her to take treatment with a psychoanalyst, or at least to try her brand of sleeping pills; Gladys had been unable to tell her many of her latest worries due to Mary Ann's insistence upon resorting to the aforementioned remedies. There was a fundamental reason for Gladys' resistence to psychotherapy: superfluous expenditures did not fit into her plan to buy a piece of property.

When her crying subsided she was relatively near her house but, as if someone had whispered it in her ear, Gladys obeyed an order: take a taxi, since her body had become chilled and she could catch a cold, one of her constant fears. If at that moment she had continued on her usual walking route, she would have met an old acquaintance on the avenue: the handsome creator of the Icarus. The boy was passing through Washington—alone and pressured by all kinds of problems—where he knew Gladys lived, and whom he would have joyfully visited if he had known her address.

Already back home Gladys prepared a tuna and tomato sandwich, poured a glass of milk and said goodnight to the old couple. She turned on the television and saw two movies of the forties which did not succeed in engrossing her. At midnight she had still not fallen asleep, she had a headache and could not accept the idea of seeing a third movie. For the nth time her eyes wandered over the outlines of the furniture in the dark, the same ideas again assaulted Gladys—her triumphant and married friends—added to which was the humiliating mistake discovered in the office that day. She jumped up and turned on the television. But the silvery light hurt her retina and her headache increased. She decided to bundle up well and take a walk for a few blocks with the intention of calming her nerves. The neighborhood of cottages, with gardens that at times reached as far as the old trees on the sidewalk, was submerged in silence and darkness. Gladys breathed in the fresh air and felt instant relief. She walked to the corner in order to go around the block. She was stopped by a strong hand that covered her mouth. Gladys saw only the arm which covered by a black leather sleeve held her brutally by the waist. Through the clothes she felt his erect member, the assailant pushed her into the garden of a private house and threatened her with a bludgeon covered with prickles: she must not scream. Gladys, lying on the grass, promised to keep quiet. His face was masked, standing up he lowered his pants and showed her his member. Gladys noticed that it was much smaller than what she had imagined as the common size in all men, and when he uncovered his face she saw that his mouth was toothless and the look in his eyes lost and insane. Gladys instinctively screamed with all her might. The man hit her in the face with the bludgeon and Gladys' howl of pain succeeded in frightening the assailant, who fled when he saw lights go on in the house.

The medical care cost the young woman her savings and she even acquired a debt in order to pay for the second plastic surgery operation, very satisfactory according to her friends. The blow of the bludgeon had broken the bone forming the arch of the eyebrow. Her left eyelid had been torn and the eyeball had been destroyed. Gladys rejected the placement of a glass eye and the surgeon managed to make it look as if the eyelid seemed closed but not sunken. The victim of the accident decided to wear dark glasses permanently, and when her boss sent her to New York to help Bob during the visit of a South American industrialist to that city, the girl also made another decision.

New York

Stimulated by the news of Bob's new separation from his wife, which came after a short reconciliation, Gladys took action. At the end of a business dinner, on the second day of her New York assignment, Gladys suggested to Bob that he come up to her room when the young man accompanied her to the door of the hotel. Bob accepted and when they were in the room he kissed her apprehensively. Gladys was trembling. Bob asked her not to say anything at the office, but when he noticed that Gladys continued to tremble he asked her why she was so afraid. Gladys remained silent. Bob asked her if she was a virgin. Gladys assented and the young man wished her good-night saying that they would discuss the matter the next day.

Alone in her room Gladys continued to tremble. She pressed the button for room service and a fat old man appeared saying that at that time of the night he could not comply with her request for a double scotch. Gladys had to go down to the hotel bar on the ground floor. At the bar was an impeccably dressed gentleman with a kind face:

when Gladys' lighter failed he came over to her and asked if she worked at the United Nations. Gladys felt tempted to lie and said yes. The gentleman spoke to her about his business trips to Mexico and about the intensely cold weather he had to put up with in Chicago, his home town. When Gladys got up, the gentleman accompanied her to the door of her room. Once there he took her hand and kissed it tenderly. Gladys felt that something was thawing inside her chest, and from that piece of ice she seemed to carry under her ribs abundant tears flowed: the room was in perfect order, the gentleman sat her on his knees and covered her with his typically long Anglo-Saxon arms. They began to feel warm, the gentleman took off some of Gladys' clothing and laid her on the bed. With her eyesight diminished but still keen Gladys followed all the gentleman's movements. He put out the light, took off his own clothes and finished undressing the girl, who at that moment felt drained and incapable of reacting.

The next day neither Bob nor Gladys, when they met for lunch with the South American industrialist, brought up the subject of female virginity, and two weeks later the girl handed in her resignation to the company in Washington in order to move permanently to New York City, where she obtained a similar job. She rented a small apartment and twice a month she saw her friend from Chicago who soon proved to be surprisingly similar to Mary Ann in regard to his total confidence in psychoanalytical treatment. Gladys was also surprised to notice that her sexual enjoyment was limited, since she never reached the necessary climax, but she was afraid of letting her friend know because she could guess the answer: psychoanalytical treatment would help her, but she was still determined to avoid that expense. A few months later the gentleman was sent to Texas for a period of ten months and obligingly suggested that Gladys follow him since his wife would stay in Chicago with the rest of the family. Gladys thought that the compensations would not be worth the trouble of moving and looking for a new job, she preferred to stay in New York.

Two weeks later she noticed that despite the limited success of her meetings with the gentleman from Chicago, her constitution had become accustomed to the attack of a male body and at night certain memories, for example the cunnilinguses of which she had been the object, made her sleepless reproducing the same kind of insomnia suffered in Washington when she remembered the success of her Argentine classmates.

Nervous problems

From then on, until her return to Argentina four years later, Gladys had sexual intercourse with six men in the following order: 1) Francisco or Frank, janitor at the company where she worked, a young Puerto Rican mulatto, married and the father of three; 2) Bob, her ex-boss from Washington; 3) Lon, a black painter whom she met during a risky solitary excursion to an off-Broadway theater; 4) Danny, History student at the University of Washington, passing through New York for Easter vacation, and the bearer of a gift from Mary Ann; 5) Ricardo, an unemployed Mexican whom Gladys met in Acapulco on her vacation; 6) Pete, the husband of a next door neighbor.

The motives that led Gladys to these couplings were the following. 1) She was attracted to Frank—that is, the janitor—because she unexpectedly found herself alone with him in the basement of the building and because of the need to fill the emptiness left by her first lover, it here being necessary to point out that until a few moments before embracing him she had not thought that such a thing could ever happen. It was Friday afternoon and both had to remain after hours to dispatch an urgent order to South America. Gladys wrote out the invoices and bilingual labels while Frank did the packing. Their conversations previous to that afternoon had never lasted more than five minutes, but at 7:30 they had to eat together in order to regain their energy and Frank invited her to a beer; moments later Gladys reached a full orgasm for the first time in her life, deducing, when she got home, that the good result had been due to a lack of expectations, and she was even reminded of a maxim of one of her high school friends, "the best parties are the improvised ones."

2) She was attracted to Bob—that is, the ex-boss—because of the combination of qualities already indicated. They had met by chance on Fifth Avenue, after months of not seeing each other, and the girl, to make herself more desirable, told him that she had married, "if not I'd invite you home so that we could relax and talk," to which Bob answered that being Saturday morning there was nobody in his office. To Bob she looked changed that morning, more sure of herself, better dressed—in fact, she had decided to spend more money on her personal appearance—, and even interesting behind her enormous dark glasses, to which it is fitting to add that Bob's impression was correct: the girl looked different ever since her objective in life—after what happened with Frank—was to repeat that moment of joy, in the arms, of course, of someone who could offer her a future. For Bob the thirty-year-old woman had promised herself to play the role of an indifferent adventuress, but upon finding herself half-naked on a couch in her ex-boss's office—he performed a skillful play of fingernails and tips upon the girl's sex organ—, she gave full rein to her emotions and confessed between embraces, kisses and caresses all her love of the past. Thus Gladys surrendered herself totally for the first time in her life and figured that little else would be needed to unchain the healthy physical reaction, but unfortunately the little she received was not enough since the young man's performance was deficient given its extreme brevity, as Bob suffered from "ejaculatio praecox" in all his exchanges.

3) She was attracted to Lon—that is, the black painter—because of his sensual African physique and the possibility of discussing art, plus the mystery of his Bohemian ex-

istence. They saw each other once a week for a year until the young man became annoyed at Gladys' reluctance to prepare meals in her apartment, and out of provisions which she bought once a week at the supermarket and kept in the refrigerator with the firm goal of making them last for seven days. Besides, a disagreement had undermined their relationship from the beginning, when Gladys showed him some of her drawings from years back and he discarded them as conventional. Lon educated Gladys sexually and made her used to regular physical satisfaction.

4) She was attracted to Danny because of his promising situation as a student, open to all the possibilities of triumph; the boy's arrival was a surprise and Mary Ann's gift, a silk Hindu scarf, highly appreciated. They immediately struck up a conversation, he wanted to know what shows and museums were good to see. Gladys mastered the subject, the boy was amazed at so much knowledge, expressed his admiration, which encouraged Gladys to talk about her neglected artistic activity. That subject led the boy to say that he sometimes posed for art students at the University because of his well-developed torso, though he was a bit bowlegged. He felt an uncontrollable desire to take off his clothes, it excited him immensely to be in a room with an older woman and he asked Gladys if he could take off his shirt so that she could offer an opinion about his modeling qualities. Gladys assented, he took off his shirt and walked around the room, told her that he admired her for her vast knowledge of art. Suddenly he took Gladys' hand and put it on his left biceps so that she could assess its hardness. More than anything Gladys thought that this young man had his whole life ahead of him, and that with good guidance he could have a brilliant career since he had an obvious quality: he knew how to listen and was interested in everything, the arts, sports, history. With Danny Gladys achieved in a single meeting her most satisfactory relationship to date, since it combined a romantic atmosphere and prospects of a happy future, with a fulfilling physical act. The only unpleasant moment in the

43

brief episode took place when the boy suggested a visit to the Museum of Modern Art: Gladys refused to go and gave as an explanation that "I don't go to museums and galleries anymore because they depress me."

5) She was attracted to Ricardo—that is, the Mexican—because of the young man's good looks and seductive talents, he made her believe that he was madly in love with her. The Mexican replaced the guide who had to take a mixed group of tourists on a nightclub tour called "Acapulco by Night," and he was happy that Gladys could speak Spanish and help him communicate with the rest of the lot. He told her that he didn't have a job, that he had started medical school and had not been able to continue for financial reasons. He also spoke to her at length about his dream of emigrating to the USA where he could work and study at the same time. Gladys was determined to have a holiday adventure with him but she did not foresee the possibility of falling in love, on the contrary, she was against prolonging the idyll, with such annoyances as letter writing, making dates for the following year, developing unfounded hopes, etc. In spite of this, Ricardo managed to convince her in a few days that he depended upon her emotionally and thus for the first time in her life Gladys lived through all the ups and downs of an apparently reciprocated love. The fifteen days in Acapulco fulfilled all her romantic aspirations and the following two months of separation made her conceive boundless illusions of a joyous rendezvous.

When there began to be delays in the visa transactions, insomnia and her firm decision not to see other men threatened her emotional stability. In fact, every night when she went to bed she could not avoid having erotic memories which excited her and prevented her from sleeping, all that if she didn't take a small dose of sleeping pills. Four months later his application for immigration to the USA, supported by her,—she was to deposit a security of one thousand dollars—received a negative response from the United States consulate in Acapulco due to the candidate's bad record. Gladys' second and last trip to Acapulco, eight months later, showed her that the relationship had ended since when she suggested remaining to live in Mexico—now that he couldn't enter the USA—the young man was against it and, besides, made himself scarce.

Back in New York Gladys attempted to renew her relationship with Lon the painter, but in the interim he had married; on the following weekend Gladys flew to Washington with the pretext of visiting Mary Ann and, when she made a date with Danny the student, he showed up with a girlfriend.

6) She was attracted to Pete—that is, the neighbor—, because of the anguished need to forget Ricardo's treachery. It had been weeks since an opportunity of meeting representatives of the opposite sex had come up, until one day when she missed work she went down to the basement to do her laundry in the washing machine and started up a conversation with a neighbor. Gladys remembered that he was one of the most impolite and ill-natured tenants in the building, whom she was always afraid of meeting in the elevator, but the conversation developed rapidly and pleasantly; the neighbor—the whole day confined to his apartment doing translations while his wife worked at an office—spiritedly told about his fight against alcohol, for example the temptation to go down to a bar assaulted him more than once during his long day's work in the lonely company of a text in a foreign language and two dictionaries; upon saying good-by he asked Gladys to invite him up to her apartment for just one drink, and she answered that unfortunately she had to go out right away.

The next day the neighbor knocked on the girl's door and she couldn't avoid opening it, she debated between the desire of having company and the fear of unpleasant complications with a married neighbor; they had a shot of whiskey and made love. But in the following visits—once or twice a week—the neighbor increased the amount of whiskey and displaced his main object of pleasure; one morning on her way to work Gladys met, on the elevator, the neighbor's wife who told her to try not to have liquor in her house, said good-by with sad fatigue, and disappeared. Gladys hid the whiskey, and during the neighbor's following and last visit he apologized for his poor behavior, looked at the shelf where the whiskey and soda were usually to be found—the desired bottle had disappeared—and left a few minutes later in embarrassment.

By then Gladys discovered that the mild tranquilizers which had helped her during the long months of waiting for the visa no longer had any effect on her. She would be particularly upset at the sight of good-looking couples in affectionate poses on the street, when on her way back to the apartment, comfortably warm because of central heating. She'd find it clean and neat, since unable to sleep beyond five in the morning she'd busy herself by putting everything in order until it was time to go to the office.

But during that winter the situation got worse, the lack of sleep produced growing headaches and she had to increase the dosage of tranquilizers, though the quantity necessary to make her rest the whole night made her sleepy for the rest of the day and in the office she had to make a painful effort to concentrate. She found herself forced to ask for frequent leaves; confined to her apartment she tried to recover her strength by resting and watching television. In the spring she had to go to a hospital for fear that the emotional crisis would continue and that the obsession of throwing herself out the window would lead her to an act which she repudiated.

A little after, and under medical advice, her mother arrived in New York from Buenos Aires and convinced the girl to return home. From Buenos Aires they went directly to White Beach, a small seaside resort where Clara Evelia had obtained on loan the house of wealthy friends for an indefinite period of time. It was then the month of May 1968.

IV

English officer: (aboard the Shanghai-Peking Express) You have changed, Magdalen. You've changed a lot.

Marlene Dietrich: (distant, looking out the window at the fleeting landscapes) Have I lost my looks?

English officer: No . . . you're more beautiful than ever.

Marlene Dietrich: Well, how have I changed?

English officer: I don't know . . . I wish I could describe it.

Marlene Dietrich: Well . . . I've changed my name.

English officer: Married?

Marlene Dietrich: (ironic and bitter) No . . . It took more than one man to change my name to (she caresses the black feathers of her coiffure) . . . Shanghai Lily.

English officer: (with poorly disguised indignation) So you're Shanghai Lily.

Marlene Dietrich: The notorious White Flower of China. You might have heard what they say about me, and what's even worse . . . you believed it.

(from *The Shanghai Express*, Paramount Pictures)

the horizontal latch, if the door is closed the latch remains horizontal and the door stays within its frame until an imperceptible downward movement of the latch can alert whoever is in this bed looking toward the door. If the window is open and some wind is blowing, even without looking toward the door the sudden air current would mean that without asking permission someone is entering this room. Two blocks away the sea, the sidewalks, the front garden with the parlor overlooking it, then the bedrooms, the bathroom, and the kitchen and the abandoned courtyard, two pine trees planted a few years ago. A house where two women live alone, the other is the mother and she is fast asleep in the next room. She does not hear the silent footsteps. Forgetting, neglecting to lock the front door perhaps has been intentional but nobody can prove it, because psychologists cannot read their patients' minds, sometimes they can be right, but if somebody asked them to declare it in court, under oath, those psychologists would abstain. Neither can their patients be sure of having forgotten to lock the front door motivated by some shameful impulse. The front door cannot be seen from the bed, the first warning comes from the bedroom door latch which changes position and in the frame of the door a figure appears. Neither does the slight creaking of the hinges wake up the mother. On this beach during the winter one always hears the same wind, the needles of the pine trees hum and despite its plaintive tone the wind can help one to sleep, or to cover the sound of the footsteps: he puts a finger on his lips and asks me to please be quiet, now he is so close that his words cannot be heard in the next room, he is whispering in my ear. Next to the bed, the lambskin to step onto when the daughter stands in her barefeet, long treaded grey white hairs and with a thick comb the newly washed and whitened lambskin can be groomed again and getting out of bed with clean feet the soft wool is not the same temperature as the tiles. Under the glass of the night

table the map of America with the itinerary Buenos Aires–
Washington–New York–Los Angeles–San Francisco–New
York–Mexico–Acapulco–New York–Buenos Aires marked
in red pencil, half-covered by a lamprest as white as ivory,
with two branches for their respective bulbs hidden by the
opaque raw silk shade, and two porcelain flowers that
adorn the lamprest with small leaves on their sides. The
flowers are porcelain like the lamprest and they burst from
the lamprest which is the stem of a plant and the flowers
burst out a little before the stem spreads into two
branches. The flowers and leaves, ivory white, shine like
porcelain, after they're dusted with a damp rag no more
dust is left in the cracks and the flowers can be licked,
they have no taste, a bottle of lotion in the closet, the
applicator of the same glass with four or five drops of lotion that fall onto the porcelain flowers, they smell like the
flowers in a strange garden, but upon licking and kissing
them the lotion burns on the tongue and reminds one of
the methyl alcohol for heaters, those flowers are only for
looking, or their scent, after they're perfumed, for deep
inhaling. One can't hear what he's whispering, in a very
low voice so that it can't be heard in the other room, from
one moment to the next instead of whispering he's going
to kiss my ear, for fear that the kiss will be violent one
can't pay attention to what he's saying. Better not to listen
because maybe he's announcing his departure will be that
same afternoon, if it wasn't so cold on this beach perhaps
he'd forget his obligations and stay one or two or three
days hidden behind the pine trees in the garden, or in the
closet. But since the temperature outside is so low he
should hurry and come in, his right hand holds a gift from
Mary Ann: untying the silk bow, the cellophane crackles
upon unfolding the ends in triangular folds, the thick mint
green and white striped waxed paper, the box is square
and for the moment nothing reveals the contents because
the skin on his face shows traces of acne and his underwear is not visible under the heavy jacket with anchor
buttons, the sweater vest of imitation cashmere, the

49

checked shirt, and flannel pants. On the other hand, for women in their thirties it is a day apparently the same as any other day, is this New York City the largest in the world? in the automat for a coin in the slot a stream of dark caramel-colored soda in a tall colorless glass the bubbles may explode not only in the glass but also in the mouth and throat, two large coins in another slot and one opens the little door of the tuna fish sandwich, a leaf of lettuce and two slices of tomato, a slight touch of mayonnaise. Chewing it little by little one can swallow it without the slightest inconvenience, but if a murderer's hand opened the victim's mouth by force, inserting the whole sandwich with all his criminal ferocity into her throat he would succeed in fatally asphyxiating her. Trees breathe through their leaves, and, as is to be expected at this time of the year, tender buds can be seen everywhere. A few blocks from there the apartment building covering a whole block with twenty floors and thirty apartments on each floor, two times three is six that makes six hundred, and if the boy with the present in his hand has lost his note with the apartment number he'll have to ask the superintendent of the building who may have gone out.* It doesn't matter if the elevator doesn't work because the young man's body is in good shape from basketball, broad jump and swimming, although this semester he had to concentrate on studying the reasons that made presidents govern in different ways. His brief vacation begins with a visit to the Museum of the City of New York, but the time schedule of that seldom frequented museum is not in the newspaper. A few days more and all the ladies in the United States will come out on the streets with new hats covered with flowers in lilac or pink tones and when taking off his jacket, sweater vest, shirt, pants, socks, shoes, his printed underpants can be hiding very recent buds of a vine similar to ivy. When young blood is too rich acne can sprout, which produces repulsion and does not invite caresses and even less, kiss-

* Gladys slides a hand under her nightgown and caresses her thighs.

es. But when from his own flesh light green buds sprout, soon a tangle of new leaves forms, the ivy covering the austere buildings of the University is somber in comparison with the soft light green thornless bramble that with skillful movements can be torn from torso, legs, and arms, without a drop of blood leaking from the tender truncated reeds. Which is why it is necessary to guess exactly where the animal flesh becomes vegetal, but touching certain places would imply a total lack of modesty.* The skin, finally uncovered, is pale pink, it's been months since the sun has touched it, while the bramble was a very light green. The curved spine because of many hours of study, on the other hand she watches old movies on television sitting up straight so as not to curve her spine. The first kiss is not on the ear, it is on her dry lips, soda drinking lips; fresh fruit juice is sometimes the only beverage that appeases thirst, quiet! . . . don't speak, not even in a whisper, don't you hear those footsteps? the mother has already gotten up, she will knock on the closed door and he hides in the bed, the rough sheets made by the depressing local industry, soft sheets that used to caress me, New York sheets, these are not the same, are they? wrapped in rough sheets with an infamous color because they don't know how to make dye in this country, he doesn't find out because he didn't reach the bed, he looks from the door, it is possible that behind some tree he may wait for sundown to attempt another assault upon the room of a victim who doesn't succeed in calling for help

—Gladys, get dressed, they're coming to get us . . .
—I'm coming.
—Were you able to get some sleep?
—Yes.
—Wonderful! . . . Fix yourself up a little. It seems to me that out of consideration for them you shouldn't look sloppy, don't you think I'm right?

* Gladys brings her hand up to her pubic hair.

51

—. . . Okay, but I'm not going to play, I'm taking something to read, but don't worry, I won't get bored.

—If we set up a canasta game for couples and you have no choice but to play, please . . .

—Is it very cold out?

in White Beach after siesta picking up her mother to play canasta, the school teacher and her husband the veterinarian sleep all night in the same large bed, probably in the nude, and the land surveyor and his wife also at the canasta game today and the school teacher won with her partner, the land surveyor, "Clara, your daughter's getting bored!" someone said, the veterinarian's wife said it yesterday. Before going to sleep she checks behind the furniture, under the bed, inside the closet, for fear of criminals. She gets into bed once she's absolutely sure that there are no strangers in the house and that doors and windows are tightly shut. If the wind didn't shake the pine trees there wouldn't be any humming and having had three glasses of wine it would be bad to take a pill in order to fall asleep. Alcohol with sleeping pills can kill, there is no television set in the borrowed house, and the drawing paper now in place on the easel in the da Vinci Institute the naked model,* with longshoreman's arms, goes up on the platform: around each nipple a circle of black hair, the circles touch, from the center of the chest descends an arrow of increasingly curlier black hair which touches the navel and further below the arrow fuses with the underbrush of hell. Tall black thick flames if you want to catch a flame with your hand the cries of pain and in your hand you catch nothing, when the flames are hair they can be touched and it is possible to sink your fingers into the undergrowth of hair and when the sun comes out the next day the hands are mere bones covered partially by sores with yellow centers and pink, then red grooves, growing darker and darker toward the edges, black, the red flower

* Gladys introduces the tip of a finger into her sex organ, getting a cold sensation.

called the federal star, red dahlias, deep violet lilies, the flower which almost seems to be flesh is the orchid, lines, forms, volumes which cannot be drawn, because they're ugly, grotesque *: a twisted pipe, furrowed with veins, its tip a dart or a poisoned Indian arrow, two grotesque hanging spheres the shame of creation, nature's mistake, the Greek sculptors forced to reduce the devil's flesh to infantile, graceful, discreet dimensions, drawing him standing, bending a knee, his arms stretched out in a horizontal line: the waning moon through the window throws a light in order to sketch the contours of the model standing in the middle of the bedroom, there is less light than in the Institute. A woman sketches him with little precision in charcoal on the drawing paper, the attempts seldom succeed, only the blurry contour and on another sheet of finer grain it is possible to draw quite neatly, filling the whole space, his head.** Without resting the hand and holding the charcoal by its lower end the lineal dashes of the wild hair, symbol of his as yet uncultivated intellect. Pressing the charcoal a little harder she draws the wavy and premature wrinkles on his forehead because his wife is in the hospital and nobody is taking care of his son, a few months old. Holding the charcoal even more firmly she traces his eyebrows and the somewhat contracted brow because his bricklayer's job brings in barely enough to eat and raising the hand a bit more, very steadily, she sketches the two almost parallel curves of the eyelid and where those lines flow into each other stretching into eyelashes one must dilute and erase the idea of suicide, because young men don't think about that. On the other hand the iris of the eye and the pupils are to be shadowed transparently like wet glass, which looks like the sad eyes of good men when they think of all that has gone wrong in their life. The floor boards creak in this old tenement, as they do every night under his footsteps, one can hear him

* Gladys tries to visualize the model's erect sex organ, without succeeding.
** Gladys achieves a hint of pleasure.

go up the stairs, besides today the rain drums against the sheet metal walls.* He comes in, takes off his worker's cap, today the walls are damp since the kerosene heater has been turned on, by whom? and has heated up the room, an act of charity. The little boy sleeps, doesn't cry, the worker doesn't ask why that woman is there, he sees a hot dish on the table and devours it in a few bites while two white hands wash the dishes. Her back is turned to him, in silence. He belches unintentionally and does not think to excuse himself but he thanks her for her selflessness. The response is not ambiguous: she is there for the satisfaction of helping whoever deserves it, and immediately informs him that, her task finished, she will leave even though it's raining, to come back the next afternoon . . . and she begins to dry the dishes. The rain keeps drumming down, with her back to him it's hard to see what he's doing, fork and knife were placed noisily on the plate. Suddenly one hears his footsteps go toward the door, he locks it. One hears his shoes fall against the floor of worm-eaten boards, then the belt-buckle which is unfastened, next the coins in his pockets clink together as he throws his pants against the back of a chair. The rooms of the tenement are crowded together and a cry for help would be heard despite the storm but if the wind from the sea hummed like last week maybe not. For an apron she had put on an old dish rag, she takes it off. Also her dress so as not to wrinkle it when she lies down on the bed to rest a moment, occupying the place of the absent sick woman. She knows that he is naked under the sheet because the coarse material allows one to guess his man's or animal's form. What one most fears is an attack that would be as brutal as it would be sudden but one doesn't hear a single word, they do not brush against each other, silence, he sits up gradually, looks in this direction and after a moment of confusion, haunted by misfortune, he rests his head on a silky white shoulder, his breath warms the bras-

* In Gladys, the pleasurable sensation produced by her own finger increases.

siere and the slip.* Since evils don't last a whole lifetime one must have patience, the baby will grow up healthy and in time his wife will also get better, work is the law of life and his bosses will notice that he is a good worker and will raise his salary, they will give him more responsibility; a simple man, who hears those calm words of encouragement, suddenly sees clearer, breathes deep, looks to either side, not straight ahead, while he seizes a white arm, the other white arm, and holds me still, but does the skin of a bricklayer who hasn't bathed smell bad? ** do the men who don't have hot water in their houses bathe? how does their hair feel to the touch? soft or dirty and sticky? what was the house of a model who was also a bricklayer like? very cold in the winter, and has the wife of the bricklayer-model already died? was it his fault she was taken to the hospital? the woman who replaces her lies defenseless on the bed, her flesh does not respond to the offender's stimulation, the turned-off stove no longer radiates heat and the cold filters in through the sheets of metal, the frozen air enfolds the naked bodies. Was siesta time pleasurable beneath the tropical sun? fruit ripens so quickly, the fruit which exists only there, impossible to imagine the taste of unknown tropical fruits *** and what future is there for an educated woman, beside that primitive married man with children? subjects in common? long dinners in total silence, the desire to drink the juice of gigantic, sweet limes, and to swallow the pulp of ripe mangos, in a temperate country to the north of the tropic of Cancer, with a whole family tradition, an educated man with a future,**** exceptionally handsome, with short hair but some waves on top of his skull where babies have a soft spot in the bone that can be caressed, a thin fuzz grows there and people are tempted to touch and see that the bone is soft, but

* Gladys finds herself forced to stop the action of her finger in order to avoid a hurried orgasm.
** Gladys in vain tries to resume her interrupted pleasure.
*** Gladys no longer feels any pleasure.
**** Gladys presses her nail against her skin, as Bob did before possessing her.

nobody dares, if someone dared he could press down the top of a baby's skull * some thousandth of an inch permanently deforming his character, his fate that is already written in his character. A pact of silence, in exchange for what? "don't ever call me on the phone, divorce suits are very long and according to the laws in this State they can accuse me of adultery." The pact means that he will answer only a special message, and only the flesh close to becoming mortally chilled is capable of emitting the call on a telepathic wave, but the divorced man goes out at night because he needs to look for company and he stays home because the next day he must get up early to go to the office, what kind of life does a divorced man lead? ** her television is turned off and the glass screen only reflects the lights of the other lamps in the room but behind the glass there's a dark dead grey membrane: it is too late now, the lamps in the room give off hot slightly golden lights, New York lamps fed by an unusually rich current, what is its voltage? she doesn't want them to light her that night, moments before while alone in the dark she presses a button that injects the grey membrane with electricity, white silvery light of the dead in the only room in apartment 302, the body of a dead woman can be infused with energy by means of special electric shocks, the dead woman shudders, now standing she takes some steps and moves, brings her hand to the telephone and when he rushes to her call and knocks on the door she turns the lock and opens, and upon receiving the first—and last— kiss the visitor falls electrocuted on the synthetic rug. The dead woman looks at herself in the mirror and notices that on her lips the recently applied lipstick shines like black shoe polish, besides the facial powder tastes like chalk and does not succeed in covering the deep cracks in the skin, corroded like old dried wood, cracks on the cheeks and the edge of the jaw. He resisted coming because someone had told him that a woman with an injured eye brings bad

---

* Gladys' fingernail feels unpleasantly sharp.
** Gladys withdraws her hand from her sex organ.

luck. He has come and it is forbidden to tell of his visit, bound by the pact. The lie, telling the land surveyor's wife about how, with a valid passport, one travels from downtown New York in a helicopter to the airport, a plane to Buenos Aires airport and a limousine to White Beach because Americans prefer to save time not money: in the grey air of the seaside morning against a charcoal *sfumato* background the face is outlined in colors because one can also sketch a dead person in grey but Bob's perfect features are perfect as much for their lines as for their coloring *: blue eyes, blond or almost dark brown eyelashes and eyebrows, the complexion somewhere between pink and gold, the lips almost red, ivory teeth, pink, soft ear cartilage, the first to be bitten, he rests on the white pillow, the head sketched in all the pastel colors of the pencil box imported from Bohemia. Difficult to paint him in oils, pastel is easier, but the visitor touched the black shoe polish lips and died because of an unexpected electric shock. The cover of the book by Stekel was probably grey, and on the white pages in black letters the strange phenomenon of Ejaculatio Praecox was explained. Perhaps there were illustrations in that book, but only in black and white,** there were probably no illustrations in pastel tones. On the other hand, the travel pamphlets which advertise the island of Puerto Rico are in color. In color TV the blacks are purple rather than dark brown, as they really are in reality. Puerto Rican mulattos they say have a different hue, so they say, but every time a black man appeared on the small screen ladies thought they would never let him touch their insides: more than one shares the same shame, that white woman on a dark street the white flower symbol of charity pinned on her dress, decides to surrender to the black man because he's sad, the eyes of a forgotten ape. She wants to show him that he does not nauseate her because his arms are already encircling her, and her flesh

---

* Gladys again introduces a finger into her sex organ.
** Gladys does not succeed in resuming her pleasure and places the palms of both hands at her sides, against the mattress.

white as the bacon stored for weeks among the accumulated ice in the freezer makes way for the blackness of a gorilla who speaks to thank her for not complaining, not screaming, not calling for a doctor, with an enormous sharp knife the white bacon is cut into strips. According to the item in an old newspaper, a woman let an enormous dog or mastiff mount her,* and afterwards that woman can't ever have contact with men again because she's impregnated with odors, and men can tell that she had intercourse with animals. If the day's mail has been dispatched, if all the packages to be sent out Monday are already prepared and if they aren't expecting large orders even though it is barely three-thirty or four o'clock in the afternoon the janitor can leave work for the day because New York's Puerto Rican population has already adopted the customs of the big city.** If there are no letters in the tape recorder to type, if there are no letters from overseas to translate and if they are not expecting any telephone call of special importance the bilingual secretary can leave work early on Fridays, because it's the custom for those who have the means to leave New York on the weekends in search of rest and recreation. If on the other hand it is essential to send out an important order on Friday, even if the case had never come up before, neither the bilingual secretary nor the janitor could refuse to stay a few hours extra and help the company out of a tight spot. None of the remaining thirty-one employees will have to stay. If at seven in the evening the secretary has a voracious appetite, as a superior she should not accept the janitor's proposal because he's a mulatto. She let him go downstairs and bring back a half gallon of beer to accompany the fried food sold a few blocks away.*** It is impossible to eat spicy dishes without beer and in the fried food places in New York's Puerto Rican neighborhoods there are appetizing-looking dishes in the window: large meat *pasteles,* rolls of blackish mincemeat

* Gladys feels that the growing sweat in her armpits irritates her skin.
** Gladys's nerves quiet down after drying her armpits with a corner of the sheet.
*** Gladys almost unconsciously resumes her action.

and ground corn wrapped in boiled green cayabo leaves,
all that boils in the mouth with hot spice, chili, *mole*, and
wild peppers, and the man who eats it has thick, hot blood
especially when the secretary sits with her legs crossed
and her skirt rises more than it should.* If the secretary
begins a new subject of conversation he replies that although he works all day long carrying boxes he doesn't
have underarm odor because he uses a deodorant but the
bilingual secretary smells his beer breath, and on the
boss's couch what happens to those who drink alcohol is
that they don't think about anything, that's why many people drink, so as not to think, and sometimes it is possible
that by drinking a woman doesn't think about her own
good and if the conversation succeeds in distracting the
secretary it will be possible for her to stand the pain that
he submits her to and if he answers her with a minimum of
courtesy she can make believe the pain is passing and that
way she doesn't try to break away from his arms.** If she
tries to break away from him she would probably not succeed and instead that could double his male impetus. If
she brings up the subject of juvenile delinquency and the
advantage of his children not growing up in a slum he
probably won't answer because he doesn't like to talk
about that subject but if several moments have already
passed she is probably getting used to his bigness and
suggests accompanying him to the free English courses
given in all the neighborhoods of New York, because by
making a sacrifice every day after work he could leave
behind his limited condition as an unskilled worker, finish
school which he had never done, be a white-collar rather
than a blue-collar worker. But he replies that he makes
more lifting heavy weights than she does typing in two different languages, because in the United States physical
labor is well paid. And then all she can do is close her
eyes because on the island where he comes from the sun

* Gladys feels a growing pleasure.
** Gladys succeeds in remembering the exact sensation produced by
Frank's large member.

59

on the beach * is as big as the whole sky and she can no longer open her eyes to look at it, she's going to be blinded if she opens her eyes, the tropical sun is burning her up and in her desperation she can nibble at him and eat his ears and nose and mustache as if they were the pies in the window of the fried food place, and the blackish *pasteles* of meat and *mole*, and the green cayabos, and the ground corn reddened by all that hot spice, now it is almost the moment when she'll be able little by little to open her eyes and look straight at the tropical sun, without blinking, and in the future they will neither be in the North Atlantic nor in the South Atlantic, naked in the Caribbean tropics they will sleep side by side ** and they will spend the day fishing and hunting for their sustenance, and won't they get bored? no, because in their free time little by little she will teach him all she knows about painting, music, literature, so that he won't feel inferior to anyone, and she will teach him to speak proper English, with the Oxford accent full of cultural echoes learned at the British Institute of Buenos Aires . . . shush! don't move! the mother has gotten up and might possibly peer in the door

—Dear . . . are you upset?
—No, I'm fine, go back to bed . . .
—I thought you were complaining . . . It's late, try to sleep.
—Okay . . .

since there is only a woman in the bed, and at her feet a lambskin, those long white hairs groomed with a thick comb, and spongy, they haven't been stepped on, only someone who deserved it would be allowed to step on them. Certain kinds of shady visitors will not be admitted, married men for instance. If the wind didn't blow in the silent night on this beach one would hear even the slight-

* Gladys feels the orgasm approaching.
** Gladys feels that the orgasm resists beginning.

60

est footstep of a man, and one cry for help would be enough to frighten away the intruder but if across continents and oceans one can transmit a Hertzian wave, the most trivial radio program, or a telegram of greetings, there is no doubt that one can also transmit the wave emanating from an immortal soul—as all souls are—, its destination a student's room in Washington University. He will only hear a special message and only the flesh close to becoming mortally chilled is capable of emitting the telepathic wave. If she can no longer tolerate the suffering of separation she will be shaken by death rattles which in turn will shake the heavens and reach his ears. Shoes can be heard but bare feet can advance and then rest on, crush, conquer the long hairs of the dead, skinned lamb, a washed, brushed, combed, perfumed pelt whenever the occupant of the room remembers and perfumes it but this time he didn't give her enough time, he arrived without warning, there were the bare feet and while her eyes move up his body that in the thick darkness is only lines without volume—lines of Greek harmony?—it is better not to greet him yet for fear of his coming near and then the lines take on their third dimension. What should she draw him as background? banners, books, tennis racquets and through the window one can see elegant Tudor-style buildings covered with ivy, but wasn't it he who went to visit her? and in the background one could see one of the highest skyscrapers in New York. If the program begins with a visit to the Museum of the City of New York it can continue with the Rouault retrospective at the Museum of Modern Art and some off-Broadway play, she knows everything and recommends only the best, and shows him photographs of a prize for the best sculpture, adding that his head offers very interesting angles for clay modeling, and the absence of facial wrinkles makes one think that because of his youth he never heard it said that one-eyed women bring bad luck.* It is not a walk in the University's

* Gladys begins to caress her pubic hair again.

English parks, it is not a stolen kiss in the main hall during a concert, it is not that he finally succeeds in possessing her in those canoes on the tame Oxford-style rivers, from the canoe she doesn't see a clear sky and branches of weeping willows,* it was lightning that in the middle of the black night dazzled her retina and she can only see colors of blood and colors of gold flow from the center of a great volcano and what destroys the skin of the mouth isn't lava, and even though it is shameful to admit, as with every woman in her too another mouth has opened, also hungry is a mouth hidden between her legs, which is finally filled to the brim with the same colors that burst from all the craters of all the volcanos still living, in the era of fire, light, heat, even if fire hurts, burns, wounds, and he also hurts and burns that mouth and tears it, and sobbing with joy and pain it is possible to notice that the flames devouring the flesh already reach the bone and the center of the chest where the soul of a one-eyed woman is all curled up and the soul succeeds in rising to the throat and escapes,** one hears a sigh which is the soul that, now free, rises and laughs from the very zenith, why?, not even she knows. Some ashes were left on the sheets and the mouth between her legs is the last live coal, which after a while goes out and disintegrates and becomes ash like the rest of that woman. Because when his desire passes he sees her grey and black in the darkness, she despite the whiteness of her skin and the pink of her mouth and breasts is only grey and black like ash to him.*** Is that possible?, because one must not confuse a noble spirit like his with others, if he's in a hurry and leaves very soon it's because he has a whole future to forge, but in his case it is not fitting to be anxious because of what may bar his way. Such anxiety disappears with the presence of a companion who will know how to complement him and enrich his

* Gladys feels the orgasm striking her suddenly and flooding her.
** Gladys exhales a deep sigh of satisfaction.
*** Gladys withdraws her hand from her sex organ and silently goes toward the bathroom.

hours, because he discovered that she knew about everything: theater, movies, painting, which doesn't mean that while he prepares for exam after exam she will stop serving coffee after coffee and the defense of his final thesis will be so brilliant that right there in the University they will offer him a professor's position, and the students will fight to go to his house because not only is he a luminary but his wife—a little older and apparently simple, always ready to cook ducks and partridges—is the most cultured, most sensitive painter and sculptor, hidden behind the shadow of her wise husband. And why is he ashamed? after making love one must always wash, with silent steps because her mother is in the room next door and can hear them, contained breathing and generous fresh water which bursts from the faucets, to erase the only trace of sadness which is on her fingers, she washes them and no trace at all remains, since in her memory he occupies all the available space and the veterinarian's wife didn't see her when she got out of bed alone to go to the bathroom to wash her hands

. . . .
. . . .

—Gladys, it's almost ten, wake up.
—Let me sleep.
—No, afterwards you're not going to be hungry and I made you something that you like.

. . . . .
—Baby, answer me, come on, meanwhile I'll make you some black coffee.
—Okay, just a few minutes more, and that's all . . .

before breakfast one forgets many things, breakfasting late takes away one's appetite for lunch. If her memory fails and she doesn't remember what exam he had to take immediately after Easter vacation the matter is probably not important, but if the veterinarian's wife asks her something similar and the answer is hard to find one can accept the excuse that with time one forgets certain things. On the other hand if only a few hours have passed it is possible to remember everything even the smallest detail.* If, the veterinarian's wife asks her even the smallest detail about the joy he gave her last night being a married woman she would not have the right to be shocked at anything and would be able to listen point by point to everything that happened. But if the veterinarian's wife says that she doesn't believe that the young man was visiting her last night—perhaps because she has found out that when the girl woke up he wasn't at her side—, there wouldn't be any proof that that student—the origin of so many illusions—has remembered her—thousands of miles away— during the early morning. The truth is that in this room no new word of his, sent by telepathy, was heard. The words remembered are those few he uttered the only day they saw each other, because about that other day in Washington when he appeared with his fiancée it isn't possible to remember anything, only the pleasant words were recorded. Although if one is going to consider the pleasant words, one may as well remember others heard in other circumstances and other places, such as Acapulco: if tomorrow, Saturday night, it is hard to fall asleep it would be possible to remember those words, and to try not to forget even the smallest detail concerning the circumstances of that precise moment. Because in Acapulco nature offers the perfect surroundings for the most diverse romantic adventures. Some with a happy ending and others not

* Gladys feels the usual headache she gets in the morning when she has overexcited herself the night before.

V

Jean Harlow: (a platinum blonde, in a Chinese prostitute's kimono, can't stand the heat of the night any
longer and goes out on the veranda of that house
lost in the jungle hundreds of miles from Saigon;
upon seeing a ferocious Bengali tiger roaming
around the place she smiles ironically) Who are you
looking for, alley cat?

The plantation's drunkard: (he puts down the bottle of gin
when he sees her nearby) I thought you had gone
back to sleep. Did that beast frighten you?

Jean Harlow: No.

The plantation's drunkard: They don't dare come any
nearer than that, you know.

Jean Harlow: I'm not used to sleeping nights anyhow

(from *Red Dust*, Metro-Goldwyn-Mayer)

Buenos Aires, May 8, 1969

An office in the Police Department. To the right, beside
a curtainless window, a modern desk with telephones,
typewriters and a tape recorder; to the left a smaller desk,
with only one telephone. One can't tell if it's day or night,

because of the closed blinds; on their respective desks, lamps are lit. A middle-aged man, carefully dressed, seated at the better desk, tries to concentrate on reading an article titled "ISRAEL ATTACKS PORT SAID" on the front page of the daily newspaper.

Assistant: (a chubby, white-haired older man, protected from the strong lamplight by an eyeshade, answers the telephone) Yes, yes miss (to his superior). For you, chief. A woman.

Officer: (he picks up the receiver) Speaking.

Voice on the telephone:

Officer: Yes, I'm listening (his eyes fall on a headline in the newspaper—"LATEST U.S. LOSSES"—and he looks over part of the text that follows without concentrating, paying attention only to the speaker)

Voice:

Officer: For information I have my assistant, I'll give you back to him.

Voice:

Officer: What kind of danger? First of all, give me your name.

Voice:

Officer: We promise absolute secrecy.

Voice:

Officer: (abrupt) Stop beating about the bush. What is the danger? what kind? (his eyes fall on a headline in the newspaper—"THE TENSION IN NORTH IRELAND INCREASES"—and part of the text that follows)

Voice:

Officer: Nobody's going to know about your call, relax. What kind of danger?

Voice:

Officer: (he signals the assistant to listen on the other telephone) Give me their names and addresses.

Voice:

Officer: The name of this man you think is dangerous, and hers.

66

Voice:

Officer: (he signals the assistant to connect the telephone line to the tape recorder) If you aren't sure, that's different. You must know that false accusations are punishable by law. Give me your name and telephone number, I'll call you back immediately.

Voice:

Officer: That man isn't going to turn against you, simply because he's not going to find out. Speak freely (his eyes fall on a headline in the newspaper—"THE OAS WILL NOT OPEN ITS DOORS TO COMMUNISM"—and part of the text that follows)

Voice:

Officer: If that incident happened to this guy years ago, and someone paid for it very dearly, like you say, it is a crime which should be reported. And you are hiding it, do you realize that?

Voice:

Officer: It doesn't matter that it was many years ago, the crime is there. Besides if that woman is now in danger like you say, there is even more reason. You have to co-operate with us. It is your duty as a citizen, do you understand or don't you?

Voice:

Officer: You don't want to be the witness of a new crime, you say? Well, it's simple to avoid. Tell me their names.

Voice:

Officer: At least one thing, what exactly happened years ago?

Voice:

Officer: Only a suspicion, nothing more?

Voice:

Officer: But explain it, what is it that you notice about him sometimes?

Voice:

Officer: What do you mean by a murderer's look?

Voice:

Officer: If the subject comes up every time you see him, try to get more out of him. Even if he resists.

Voice:

Officer: Okay, I understand. I don't think you're right, mind you, but I understand what you mean. In any case if he gets relief from talking to you, let him take you into his confidence, until he says more, and then call us.

Voice:

Officer: If you don't want to be a witness, or an accomplice, help us to avoid the crime. We want to protect you and that's why you should give us your names, yours and his. And the other woman's.

Voice:

Officer: This same number, you dial the number and then ask for extension 31.

Voice:

Officer: Any time, day or night (his eyes fall on a headline in the newspaper—"RUSSIA MAKES SERIOUS AC-CUSATION AGAINST PEKING"—and part of the text that follows)

Voice:

Officer: No, there are no doctors here. That's in the hands of Public Health.

Voice:

Officer: When it's a mental case?

Voice:

Officer: Psychiatrists . . . Yes, we have psychiatrists.

Voice:

Officer: Yes, a medical consultant, but the medical consultants aren't here, they aren't in the Department. If you give me your telephone we can put you in contact. So that they can call you.

Voice:

Officer: It depends on you.

Voice:

Officer: In what circles is he so well-known?

Voice:

Officer: You try to find out something about this matter that you mentioned, from years ago. Try to get the year and the month out of him, and here we'll look to see if there's something in the files. If it's possible ask him the day too.

Voice:

Officer: I have to promise you? what? (his eyes fall on a headline in the newspaper—"LA PLATA STUDENTS TEAM WON 3–1"—and part of the text that follows)

Voice:

Officer: We don't even know your name, how are we going to mention your call?

Voice:

Officer: Even if you're his only confidant, it doesn't matter. We'll invent another lead. What we need is some precise fact about the other matter, if there was a crime . . .

Voice:

Officer: Exactly. What you have to find out is that, the date, or the victim's name, if there was a victim, of theft, of whatever, of homicide.

Voice:

Officer: You're sure it wasn't for material gain?

Voice:

Officer: All that you know, afterwards we'll make it seem like we got to the accused by another lead. We promise that he won't suspect you.

Voice:

Officer: You need a license to carry arms (his eyes fall on a headline in the newspaper—"NIXON AND ROCKE-FELLER MEET"—and part of the text that follows)

Voice:

Officer: It's not bureaucracy, that's the law. To carry arms you need a license.

Voice:

Officer: It depends upon what kind of criminal he is, understand?

Voice:

Officer: Yes, you're right, there is the kind of criminal who when confronted, gets scared.

Voice:

69

Officer: Yes, psychopathic reasons, whatever you want to call them. But in these conditions, without any facts, what can I tell you? First of all, you get us the date of that crime. But wait a moment, he could have already been accused of something, tell me his name and we'll look to see if there's any file on him.

Voice:

Officer: I'd advise you to tell me his name now.

Voice:

Officer: You may regret it when it's too late, give me his name now.

Voice: (the line is cut off, the speaker has evidently hung up)

Officer: Hello . . . hello . . . (to the assistant, while he in turn is hanging up) Note down this call on the daily report, with the time, in case she calls again.

Assistant: Should I transcribe the tape?

Officer: No, don't bother. Only if this matter comes up again. But file the tape (his eyes fall on a headline— "MEETING OF GOVERNORS ENDS—MINISTER OF LABOR URGES THEM TO WORK FOR TRANS-FORMATION OF COUNTRY"—and he looks over part of the text that follows without concentrating, his attention still held by the recent telephone call).

The headlines and parts of texts that the officer read without paying attention were the following: 1) "LATEST U.S. LOSSES—Saigon, May 7 (UP)—More than 30 American helicopters were shot down or suffered accidents in South Vietnam in the last two weeks, and at least 49 allied soldiers perished in those disasters according to today's report in . . ." 2) "THE TENSION IN NORTH IRE-LAND INCREASES—Belfast, May 7 (UP) The Protestants today did not heed the new prime minister James Chi-chester-Clark's admonishings and will carry out a demonstration this weekend against the granting of major civil rights to Ireland's Catholic minority for the . . ." 3) "THE

OAS WILL NOT OPEN ITS DOORS TO COM-
MUNISM—CHILE'S PROPOSAL TO INVITE RED
COUNTRIES TO THE MEETINGS WAS REJECTED—
Washington, May 7 (UP)—Chile today proposed 'to open
the doors of the Organization of American States, OAS, to
the countries of the socialist world,' but was defeated in
her efforts by a narrow vote as the . . ." 4) "RUSSIA
MAKES SERIOUS ACCUSATION AGAINST PEKING—
Moscow, May 7 (UP)—The Soviet Union today accused
Communist China's top leader, Mao Tse-tung, of using the
Chinese 'cultural revolution' to arm his nation for a new
world war. A series of articles published by the Soviet
press accuse Mao of installing a 'monarchic' succession in
the Chinese Communist party and of using 'Soviet arms
destined for North Vietnam' against his political oppo-
nents when . . ." 5) "LA PLATA STUDENTS TEAM
WON 3-1—Last night in the province's capital the second
semi-final game for the Freedom Cup of America was
played between The Students Team of La Plata, and Catholic University, of Santiago de . . ." 6) "NIXON AND
ROCKEFELLER MEET—Washington, May 7 (UP)—The
White House today reported that President Richard M.
Nixon plans to meet with the governor of New York, Nelson Rockefeller, this weekend, before the latter initiates
his study mission to 23 Latin American countries to begin
the . . ." 7) "MEETING OF GOVERNORS ENDS—
MINISTER OF LABOR URGES THEM TO WORK FOR
TRANSFORMATION OF COUNTRY—Alta Gracia
(Córdoba) (By special correspondent) The deliberations of
the Governors' Third Conference, meeting since last Monday at the Sierra Hotel in this city, have ended with the as-
sembly that took place yesterday, beginning at 9:10 A.M.,
presided over by the President of the Argentine Republic,
Lieutenant General Juan Carlos Onganía; and with statements made by the Minister of Labor, Doctor Guillermo
Borda; by the Secretary of the National Council of Development (NACODE), Doctor José María Dagnino Pastore;

71

and by the councilman of the province of Buenos Aires, Admiral Muro de Nadal. According to informed sources, the program presented to the press Tuesday night by Doctor Díaz Colodrero proceeded without major changes. There was a statement of . . ."

VI

Lawyer: You've done a great job as the director of the Orphanage. You've solved many problems. But another one's come up. The Eldridge couple . . . wants little Sam.

Greer Garson: (her kind eyes become hard as glass) No. It was I who brought that child back to life, he loves me, and he belongs to me!

Lawyer: Yes, you brought him back to life. But he needs a home, a normal house, with parents he can consider his own. This is not a home, this is an institution.

Greer Garson: (passionately) Then I'll leave this place, I'll leave the Orphanage. I've found parents for thousands of children, now I want a child of my own! I want Sam. Here's my resignation to the Board.

Lawyer: Listen to me, the day your husband died, he told me something I never mentioned to you. He told me that he believed God had taken your own child when you were young so that thousands of homeless babies might have their chance to be loved . . . (he goes toward the door) Well, maybe Sam was wrong (he leaves without looking her in the face)

Greer Garson: (is crushed by that blow, but tries to regain her composure and goes up to the room where the

73

little orphan is sleeping, she wakes him up and holds him in her arms thirsty for affection) My darling, from now on . . . I want you to call me mama, not auntie. You and me . . . we're going away. We'll soon have a real home together.

Child: Oh, auntie . . . mommy! just the two of us? . . . a house with a fence and all?

Greer Garson: (full of illusions) A house with a fence and all! (one can hear the front doorbell ring, then Mrs. Eldridge's trembling voice in the drawing room, asking to see the director of the Orphanage. The latter feels that everything is in danger, is such a selfish act permitted? did that fence which was to separate her and the child from the world exist? Did it ever exist, will it ever exist?)

(from *Blossoms in the Dust*, Metro-Goldwyn-Mayer)

PRINCIPAL EVENTS IN LEO'S LIFE

On January 11, 1930, Leopoldo Druscovich and his wife, Agustina Latiuh Druscovich, celebrated the good news. Their daughters Amalia, fourteen years old, and Olga, seven, had already gone to bed. Dinner had been simple since Agustina had not returned from the doctor until late in the afternoon. According to the diagnosis Mrs. Druscovich had recovered her health and there were no longer any traces of anemia, but for lack of time it was impossible to prepare a celebration banquet to Mr. Druscovich's liking. The children were no longer around and the maid was washing the dishes in the kitchen. The couple savored the liqueur reserved for visitors on big occasions. Mr. Druscovich did not dare ask his wife if she had discussed with the doctor the possibility of having another child, and Mrs. Druscovich had been afraid that question would come up from the moment they had been alone in the room. Despite the fact that her husband had repeatedly asked her to discuss the matter with the doctor, she had avoided the subject during the consultation. Mrs. Druscovich was tired of clinical analyses and inquiries, her unconfessed fear was that the doctor would not advise a pregnancy and her husband would make her see another doctor. Mr. Druscovich strongly desired a male child.

When Mrs. Druscovich was finally faced with the question she was in no condition to answer objectively because her husband was fornicating her with all the tenderness of which he was capable. Mrs. Druscovich felt all her resistance crumble—her fear of exhaustion and the annoyance of readjusting the budget—and swept away by connubial passion murmured that she was there to do her master's will. He interrupted the act to take off his condom and before inserting his member in her again, deeply moved, he gave her a long and respectful kiss on the forehead. During a moment of the orgasm in which she closed her eyes, Mrs. Druscovich saw desert dunes stretch as far as a horizon which she could touch with her hand, in the horizon the air was mild, the pleasantly warm sand enveloped her feet, the stars shined in the dark blue sky without a single cloud and the soft hand which caressed the dunes was her own breath, while the dunes were her throat and the inside of her chest. The air came from her husband; if he remained at her side he could prolong that pleasure and that repose eternally.

She had the same vision twelve months later, shortly before dying, because of pneumonia against which her weakened constitution could not prevail. Beside the bed in the hospital were her husband and their eldest daughter, as well as medical attendants. The younger daughter had stayed home, helping the maid take care of her little three-month-old brother, christened with his father's name. Leopoldo Druscovich junior was brought up by the maid and his eldest sister and, according to the neighbors, spoiled by the younger sister.

Before the anniversary of his wife's death, Leopoldo Druscovich senior received an advantageous offer and sold his tanning shop. He feared the arrival of that date as if by then some other misfortune would occur and went to Mendoza to spend a few days at the home of his only brother. There he thought he made a good investment buying a honey farm, and the moment for him to return to Buenos Aires was postponed week after week. Meanwhile in the capital the sixteen-year-old daughter, Amalia, soon imposed her good administrative sense upon the household and in her hands the checks her father sent became more than adequate. But from her budget all unnecessary expenses disappeared, such as movies, ice cream, the merry-go-round, comics, and presents for birthdays and Christmas. On those dates the children received clothes or school supplies. Amalia kept the surplus money, planning to show it to her father when he came home and she was sure that he would not marry again if he found the house in order and with unexpected savings as a pleasant surprise.

But the father failed to return for a long time and when the more complaisant Olga wanted to cheer her little brother up she gave him clothes her father had left in the closet to play with: the little boy would dress up and drag the clothes all over the house. Olga would put on her dead mama's clothes and ask the maid to marry them.

Father and son

Leopoldo Druscovich junior saw his father for practically the first time when he was seven years old. He was having lunch as usual at eleven-thirty in the morning to go to class an hour later and the absence of his two sisters that morning had resulted in a menu which he dictated to the maid: two fried eggs and french fries, bad for the digestion according to Amalia. The door opened, father and uncle entered followed by the girls. The two men had shaved the evening before in Mendoza and their beards were rough, their small-town clothes were rumpled, their eyes reddened by staying up all night on a train, their breath heavy, and upon hugging the child whiffs of underarm sweat escaped jacket, vest, and soiled shirt.

They were all to be together until four in the afternoon, at which time Mr. Druscovich had to go to a hospital to be treated for a bad case of angina; the child was allowed to miss school. The father looked deep into his eyes as if searching for the hidden serpent that had bitten the departed, and asked him what he wanted to be when he grew up. The child answered that he wanted to be a flier and to marry Olga. The father then answered that brothers and sisters never married and little Leo, as they called him at home, repeated a gesture he had learned from the older boys at school when they said "I'll marry your sister, who's a hell of a blister." The gesture consisted of forming a circle with the thumb and forefinger of one hand and piercing it with the stiff forefinger of the other hand. The child had never uttered those words before, but he felt as if someone were whispering them in his ear and he could not resist the temptation of repeating them, without having any idea of what it all meant. Mr. Druscovich raised his voice, ordered the child never to say anything like that again. The child didn't understand the reason for that order and repeated that he was going to marry Olga. Amalia noticed her father's anger and gave the child a hard slap to silence him.

During the grownups' lunch Leo was allowed to go play on the sidewalk. Leo went out and across the street he saw a woman in a white apron go by. She was one of the teachers at school. Leo thought that she might see him and tell his teacher that a certain child had missed school without being sick. Immediately he went upstairs to the apartment, but a few steps from the dining room he stopped, he could hear them talking about him at the table. The girls told Mr. Druscovich the most notorious anecdotes about the child, and they laughed affectionately, but Leo felt humiliated by his sisters' and father's complicity. Among other things they commented that: a) evidently Leo would be a good businessman because his sisters' dolls and other

77

old toys disappeared periodically and Leo would appear with lead soldiers, busted balls, toy guns, all on the basis of exchanges carried out on the sidewalk or in the square; b) a friend of the family—Amalia preferred not to indicate that it was her suitor—had taught Leo boxing, and on one occasion in which Olga had attempted to slap the child he not only intercepted her blow but had forcefully thrust his closed fist at his sister's stomach, cutting short her breath; c) they'd tell Leo that he should be a good boy because in Mendoza his father could see his dead mother who'd come down from heaven and he'd tell her everything, to which the child one day answered that if his mother came down from heaven one day to Buenos Aires, he'd ask her to take him to see the planes in the sky from close up.

A little later Amalia scolded the maid for giving the child fried eggs which he vomited in the bathroom. Before leaving for the hospital Amalia put Leo to bed with a hot water bottle on his feet. Olga stayed home to take care of him. Before going out, the father kissed the child tenderly and whispered to him that men could say dirty words, but never in front of women, and he winked at him. Leo didn't at all understand what was being said to him; the only thing he could think of was that they were ready to go out and he would stay home to play with Olga.

Olga and Leo

Olga was fifteen years old and knew all the games imaginable, thought Leo. There was one game he liked even better than playing ghosts. It was a game that took place at night when Olga put Leo to bed, or during the day, if the little boy was in bed sick. The game was as follows: Olga would say "Incey wincey spider, climbed up the water spout . . ." and with the tips of her middle and index finger she would drum upon the child's wrist all the way to his armpit and there tickle him, the child would twist and turn and both would laugh, but the climax of the game would come afterwards, when Olga would begin to drum along the child's foot and then go up to the knee, where she would pause, to then continue her climb along the thigh until reaching the pink infantile groin where the drumming would multiply and Olga would exclaim ". . . and the incey wincey spider found a little mouse and cried wee wee wee, all the way home . . .," to which the tickling on the belly continued, ". . . but then the incey wincey spider came back again and saw that it wasn't a little mouse, it was a little bell, and she began to ring the bell, ring-a-ring-a-ring . . .," and Olga would tug at the small virile member, making the child laugh convulsively.

Leo patiently waited for his sister to finish talking on the telephone with a high school friend who was bringing her up to date on everything that happened at school during her day's absence. Olga hung up and went to look at herself in the bathroom mirror. Leo called her in to play. Olga answered that they would play at reading stories. Without knowing why, Leo blushed and said he wanted to play incey wincey spider. Olga answered no, because their Daddy would get angry. Leo did not dare insist, he felt in his mouth traces of gastric juice and instead of holding in the fecal material that suddenly descended his intestines, trembling with rage he yielded to the uncontrollable impulse of voiding in the bed. Olga refused to clean it up, and while the maid changed his sheets Leo told her that his sister did not want to play incey wincey spider any more. The maid laughingly suggested that he ring Olga's little bell, Leo went running to the teenager and tried to put his hand under her skirt. Olga moved away and told him that he was a foul-mouthed, disobedient little boy, and that's why she wouldn't play with him anymore.

When Amalia came home later she didn't respond to his greeting and went running to her room to cry. The doctors had referred to her father's health in not very encouraging terms, but the child thought his sister was crying because he had behaved badly. Later, during the night, in his hospital room Mr. Druscovich felt remorse for having left his daughters alone so long—he found them dressed with little modesty, in his opinion, and with too much make-up on—and he pleaded in silence to his dead wife for help, he needed her advice, while in the apartment Amalia cried grief-stricken because of the diagnosis and Leo cried to repent for his disobedience. Olga and the maid were sleeping.

The next day Leo peeked through the bathroom keyhole and saw Olga naked for the first time; he dared to comment on the event only to the maid. "Olga has a little plant." The maid laughed out loud and told the sisters. Amalia, angry, told Olga that as punishment that weekend she would not give her money for the movies and that if she saw them playing again she'd tell their father the whole thing. Olga let out her anger by giving Leo a hard slap. Amalia in turn told the child, "You deserve it, with poor Daddy so sick and you still behaving like a bad boy. Oh, Leo, you're very little but we all have to pray for Daddy to get well." Mr. Druscovich returned to Mendoza a week later and passed away in his brother's house, because of the tracheal cancer discovered during his stay at the hospital.

Teenage problems

a) Leo stopped taking communion at fourteen, when he became ashamed of talking about his masturbating during confession.

b) Because of his premature development he was one of the strongest boys in his class and his very presence commanded respect. Besides, because of the size of his sex organ he was admired and celebrated among his friends, who made him show himself each time a new student entered the school. Leo also had a reputation for being a protector of the weaker boys; that's why nobody understood his reaction when a sickly classmate he was close to said as a joke during one recreation period that the young History teacher hadn't given Leo a failing mark because she had the "hots" for him. Leo hit him hard, without apparent

80

motive. Full of regrets he fled from school and was almost expelled because of that.

c) At age sixteen with some classmates he went to a construction site where a prostitute and her manager were waiting for them. It was the first time that Leo was going to have sexual intercourse and he became inhibited when he got near the woman; he came out of the room and asked the manager to return his money, which the man refused giving Leo a tongue-lashing; to his friends' amazement the boy did not respond to the abuse and walked away crestfallen.

d) That same year a classmate took Leo to a meeting, in the home of an ex-professor of the university—dismissed for his socialist leanings—, during which General Perón's recently elected government was passionately accused of Nazism. Leo found that these accusations had a firm basis and frequented those weekly meetings for a while, though he was worried about his inability to concentrate on what was being discussed.

e) At eighteen he entered the Graduate School of Architecture. In class he had a hard time following the professors' lectures and he couldn't manage to take complete notes. Despite his efforts, his mind would wander right in the middle of class and he feared that the reason was the masturbation he could not seem to avoid each night. He'd go to bed and the erection would anticipate the thought: the thought was always the same, a certain incident in a gymnasium of the Ministry of Education. It had happened the year before, he had stayed late doing pull-ups and went to take a shower after all his classmates had already gone; he realized he had forgotten the soap when he was already undressed, he looked on the floor and didn't find any remains of it. He remembered that a few steps away was the girls' shower, deserted. He risked crossing the corridor. He found a half-melted piece of white soap. Also, in a corner lay a forgotten bag. He yielded to his curiosity and opened it, it contained a woman's gym school outfit. He heard footsteps, the door had been left open and a young girl entered unawares. They both stood still, the young girl looked at Leo's face and against her will her eyes descended to his virile member. She immediately went out and from the outside asked him with a choked voice to hand her the bag. Leo's member was already erect. He didn't know if he should go out and show himself to the girl or simply stick his arm through the partially opened door. He hesitated a moment, holding his body against the wall. He opened the door slightly and stuck out his arm with the bag. The girl's footsteps ran away quickly. But every night Leo would again feel her eyes on his member and he could not forgive himself for having let her escape. He wallowed in bed remorsefully and to calm himself he'd imagine in many different ways the development of the scene, which would invariably end in a bloody deflowering. Leo would close his eyes and after a while his semen would mix in his thoughts with the girl's blood.

f) The demands of the university were much greater than those of public high school and one day Leo decided to ask for assistance in completing his notes after class. It was a girl who had already looked at him several times in the corridors, certainly not the prettiest in the class, she dressed poorly, was slightly heavy and her teeth had greenish stains. The one Leo coveted was Carola, the most attractive and elegant, a girl with money, but he approached the one who had shown interest in him and asked for help in completing the notes for that morning. They decided to study together in her house sometime. That day Leo overcame the repugnance that her teeth gave him, Susana was her name, and he kissed her. The grandmother was in the other room, but Leo tried anyway to lift up her skirt. Susana ordered him to leave, Leo got up to go and Susana laughing mockingly told him to come sit down beside her again. "I see that you're a good boy," Susana added and Leo slapped her hard on the cheek with the back of his hand, led by an impulse that he didn't understand. Susana began to murmur insults, between muffled sobs so as not to alarm her grandmother. Leo threw himself on top of her and began to kiss her violently. The more Susana insulted him, the more desire he felt: he took the girl's hand by force and put it on his erect member, he lifted her skirt. Susana held on to her underpants to prevent him from pulling them down. Inflamed with passion, Leo opened three buttons of his fly and placed his organ between Susana's thighs. Thus he reached orgasm. This mock sex act was repeated several times without major variations, until one day when entering Susana's house and finding that the two of them were alone Leo felt a strange displeasure. They sat down to study and the usual maneuver began again: with surprise Leo could feel that Susana was not wearing underpants. Immediately his erection subsided. He felt ill and went to the bathroom to vomit. When he came out of the bathroom he saw that Susana was lying on her grandmother's bed. Susana spoke in a honeyed voice: "I want to be yours, Leo. Grandma went to see a sick relative in Mercedes and she's not coming back till tomorrow." Leo lay undressed beside Susana but he could not get an erection. At midnight he woke up and was able to penetrate Susana. He felt contempt for her upon finishing the act, and promised himself never to see her again.

Leo's youth

The next day repulsion was replaced by the usual desire and while they studied Leo put his hand inside Susana's underpants. For fear of the grandmother they had to go out on the street and on a dark sidewalk they fornicated again, standing up.

When Leo returned home—the same apartment where he continued living with Amalia, Olga, and the latter's husband—he found his brother-in-law alone, reading the newspaper under the lamp in the living room. The latter told Leo that the sisters had gone to the movies and he was about to tell him the name of the film when he noticed whitish stains on the young man's pants. He scolded him for being careless, since those stains would have looked truly obscene in his sisters' eyes. Leo went to the bathroom immediately, took off his pants and rubbed the stains with a damp brush; his brother-in-law's reprimand, instead of bothering him, had unleashed his sensuality again, and this time more intensely than with the girl on the dark street. Leo put his pants on again but the erection didn't disappear. His member marked a straight line inside his pants. The boy waited a moment but the situation didn't change, and he could not hold back the parade of erotic images that passed through his mind: the shower room girl, Carola, the naked girls in the documentary films *Syphilis, the Hell of Sex* and *The Way We're Born*. Faced with the impossibility of passing his brother-in-law in that condition he took his pants down again and masturbated, submerged in the hot steam emanating from his skin. Upon reaching orgasm he imagined that Susana's grandmother opened the hall door of the vestibule where the couple was fornicating, and due to the surprise Leo took his member out of the vagina, thus frightening the grandmother who looked upon said object as a weapon of the devil. The orgasm over, Leo had the impression of having enjoyed it fully for the first time in his life, and he decided that Susana's vagina had been the source of his satisfaction.

The next day Leo went to the weekly meeting at the socialist professor's home and his usual companion told him that he was tired of hearing so much talk without being able to turn it into action. His companion said good-by because he was going to visit a prostitute to appease his anger. The companion was coming to a corner when Leo caught up with him; together they entered the apartment occupied by the doorman of a new building, the doorman was the prostitute's manager. First his friend went into the bedroom, fifteen minutes later Leo. The prostitute had a look of fatigue and neglect, she asked Leo to finish quickly because she was in a hurry. When Leo penetrated her she began to complain and accuse him of being brutal, "You all think that whores have a big box, don't you know that a whore can be narrow?" Leo was inflamed with passion, the prostitute again urged him to hurry. Leo finished inserting his member by means of a dry thrust and she began to shriek with pain and to ask him to be gentler. Leo could only double his brutality and the woman tried to break loose. Struggling, Leo reached a full orgasm like the one the night before in the bathroom. Filled with a new joy, he got dressed and hugging his friend he went with him to have a soda at the bar on the corner.

The following Sunday Susana phoned him wondering about his absence. She informed him that her grandmother had gone to Mercedes again; Leo went over to her house immediately. Susana opened the door for him and they went straight to the bedroom without any preliminaries. The girl did not offer the slightest resistance, Leo penetrated her without difficulty. Suddenly his erection subsided and despite all his attempts it was impossible to complete the act that afternoon. Leo never went to Susana's house again

The following Sunday, October 4, 1949, the girl called him but Leo left word for them to say he was not in, alone in his room he tried to get back to the text he was studying when a sudden erection prevented it. A half hour later he went out in the direction of the prostitute's house. He had to wait a long time for her since she had gone to visit a relative in the hospital. When the woman returned she refused to take him. Leo walked out on the street unable to answer back, he wanted to insult her but his head was a total blank. He was going to take the subway home but he stopped, as if someone had whispered in his ear and had told him to walk a few blocks instead to calm his nerves. Leo obeyed, did not go into the subway, but nothing on the street seemed to help him, the new fashion of tight skirts—accenting the backside which the passersby displayed made it impossible for him to think of anything else.

He had walked about two hundred yards along that avenue when a slight blond person of the masculine gender and with a delicate gait started to turn around repeatedly to look at Leo. With an absent-minded air he'd look at the ground each time and then swiftly at Leo's fly. The latter could not repress a new erection, and got on a bus. The person did the same. The bus was full, the person pressed against Leo's body. Leo got off and the other did the same. Leo suddenly turned around and in a gruff tone asked him what he wanted. The other said that if Leo wouldn't feel offended he could suck his member: Leo could not restrain a smile of relief, faced with the proximity of a sexual discharge. The person took courage and said that he would also let himself be penetrated, if that gave him more enjoyment. They walked in silence for several minutes; a dark lot appeared, near Leo's house. At a moment when nobody was passing by they entered, Leo opened his fly and took out his erect member. The person began to suck. Leo moved away and asked him to pull down his pants. The person refused because the member was very large. Leo grabbed his arm with all his strength and repeated the order. The person pulled down his trousers and underpants. Leo tried to penetrate him. The other struggled and tried to break loose. At one moment he managed to break away and touched his sphincter: he showed his bloodied fingers to Leo. The latter asked him to turn around, this time he would be more careful. The person refused. Leo pleaded with him to turn around. The other then began to run toward the exit among the tall weeds with his pants almost down. Halfway there he tripped and fell. Leo jumped on top of him and held him still. In a flash he inserted half of his member. The person could not hold back a howl of pain. Leo interrupted his movements. They waited a few minutes in silence, both afraid that a policeman might come, drawn by the scream. Leo could not control himself and resumed the swinging movement, covering the other's mouth with one hand. The person struggled. Leo began to feel his pleasure increasing, he caressed the hair on the nape of the person's neck. The other could not stand the torment any longer and sank his teeth with all his strength into the hand that muzzled him. Leo, desperate with pain because of the unyielding bite, saw a brick within reach of his hand and smashed it against the person's head. The other slackened the pressure of his teeth and Leo continued the coitus, the narrowness of the anal duct provided him with a new pleasure; immediately he reached a climax, murmuring "Tell me you like it, tell me you like it." He obtained no response, the person was foaming at the mouth. Leo's pleasure, already at its highest level, soon diminished, lacking a subsequent rejection on the part of the other. Terrified he ran away, there were bloodstains on his fly, he took off his jacket and carried it in his hand to cover himself. He entered a bar and looked for the number of Emergencies and Assistance. When he was sure that nobody could hear him he called and disguising his voice he informed them that there was a wounded man in the vacant lot near 3300 Paraguay Street.

Upon returning to his apartment he found his brother-in-law listening to the radio in the living room, with the volume very low so as not to disturb the others. A night soccer game was on. Leo was obviously upset and his brother-in-law asked him if he had "problems with some chick." Leo said yes. The brother-in-law replied that "the man who lets a woman treat him like a puppet is finished. Don't let them push you around ever, even if a cunt hair does have more pull than a yoke of oxen." Leo went to his room without answering. Nightmares assaulted him all night long. In the following morning's paper among the police chronicles there was a notice about a pervert found near death in a vacant lot, the apparent motive robbery. A report referring to the capture of the guilty party never appeared. Neither did the notice of the victim's death.

Political activities

The following year a friend at the university informed Leo about a demonstration they were planning in order to

87

protest against the dismissal of a professor who had stated his opposition to the President, General Perón, in class. Leo identified with the cause and in that way came into contact with members of the Communist party. The boy admired their courage and tried to join the organization, though he seemed to encounter some resistance. This was real; some of the members distrusted Leo because of his physical development, it made them think he was an agent of the secret police. The boy's persistence finally overcame their lack of confidence and in time they entrusted him with minor missions.

A few months later he was captured in compromising circumstances by the police: two plainclothesmen had followed him from the door of the printing press where they produced anti-government pamphlets. Leo became aware of them and tried to throw them off the track when it was already too late. The police mainly wanted to discover the place where Leo would leave the pamphlets, and since the boy did not inadvertently lead them there they submitted him to torture. The session took place in a police station in the southside of town; the room was small. Leo noticed a broken down cot, a table with a radio, a kind of stick and a twisted wire; immediately he fell to the floor because one of the plainclothesmen, without uttering a word, punched him in the stomach. On the radio lively country music from the riverbank provinces was playing very loud. During the second session they threatened to torture him in the groin with the cattle prodder, and the accused immediately answered the questions they put to him. Lying naked on the cot, with the corner of his lips bloodied, his eyelids blackened, Leo gave in to the terror of becoming sexually crippled. When he saw that one of the policemen was rewinding the wire, Leo wondered if the person in the lot had suffered as much before dying. He wondered if, through the torture he had just undergone, he had already paid in part for the crime committed, and he answered himself that now besides being a murderer he was an informer, tears flowing from him as thick as glycerine drops.

He then felt a growing relief, he thought of the satisfaction the Christian martyrs must have felt in the midst of their worst suffering.

The comrades he had denounced managed to escape anyway, since upon noticing Leo's delay they immediately sought refuge in the interior of the country. One of them was to play an important role in politics years later. The reticence which Leo found among his comrades back at the university made him terminate his relations with the party.

Work activities

1951—After leaving the School of Architecture because of increased difficulty in concentrating on his studies, Leo started work as layout assistant for a magazine specializing in cartoons and comic strips. He got the job on the recommendation of a friend of Olga, his younger sister. A few months later he discovered through a secretary's indiscretion—she left the accounting books within his reach—that he was really there as an apprentice without salary and that the money he was paid came out of Olga's pocket. Leo lost control of his nerves, confronted his sister and accused her of humiliating him. She answered that she had only wanted to provide him with an occupation since he had not been able to complete his university career. She moved closer to Leo and caressed him, "We had to be a mother to you, and sometimes we mothers make mistakes." Leo felt the caress was like the touch of a slimy insect, his sister had meant well, he understood it, but that did not prevent her caress from proving repulsive to him.

Leo left home that very day and settled in a cheap boarding house with clientele from the country. They were young people of both sexes from the riverbank provinces and from the north. They came to work in the new factories—created on the credit provided by the Perón government—, the young men thus escaping miserable farm wages, and the girls the unemployment which in their lands was avoided only by entering domestic service. There were two beds in the room, his roommate was already asleep when the landlady of the boarding house brought Leo in, but he woke up and they started chatting, he was a bricklayer from Corrientes. Leo told him he was unemployed and his companion answered that at his job there were openings for unskilled workers. The next morning he went to the construction site, he worked there for two months as if working out at a gymnasium. At the boarding house, Leo's position was favorable since the people from the provinces were the majority and the city people the minority—only Leo—, which led them to adopt and protect him. At the table they served him the best pieces of meat stew, they let him use the bathroom first when there were many people waiting on line, and other similar attentions. The boy felt deeply moved by this attitude.

His roommate Aureliano's simplicity was also helpful, since he had very different worries, for example sending money to his mother and four younger brothers and sisters in Corrientes. Leo considered that these problems, unlike his own, were real. When he received his second week's wages he felt an urge to give part to Aureliano, but he decided to save the surplus in case of illness and to put off the gift till the following week. Before that time was up, the people in an apartment house neighboring the construction site asked Aureliano to fix a balcony and Leo acted as assistant. Aureliano told him that with that unexpected money he was going to indulge in a pleasure: he would take a prostitute to the room, he had seen her some time ago and had not been able to forget her. The woman visited them early Thursday morning. Leo waited in the dark and silent courtyard of the boarding house. Aureliano came out radiant with joy and told him that the prostitute found Leo very handsome and offered him her favors for a few *pesos*. Leo went in, the girl was attractive and said to him, "I'm fed up with these farmers, I'll charge you half or whatever you have." Leo had difficulty getting an erection and could not reach orgasm. Two days later he received the third week's wages and did not give Aureliano the planned gift.

The following week he had an argument with another boarder for political reasons; Leo had been careful not to reveal his anti-Peronism, but he was nervous and said that the governing class needed experience and Perón's cabinet had been thrown together. Leo thought that the incident would ruin his good relationship with the group but in a few days everything was forgotten. Instead another episode, apparently unimportant, had graver consequences: one of the girl boarders, red with shame, put a letter in his hand one morning. In it she declared her love for him and made a date in her room at midnight, since her two roommates had the night shift in a factory. Leo did not appear, for fear that the meeting would be unsatisfactory and she'd tell the others. A few days later Leo came out of the bathroom and a girl who was waiting looked at him with a sour face and said that "some people think who knows what, that others aren't worth a damn and can wait an hour." Leo noticed that among the girls hostility was growing; he was afraid that the feeling would spread to the male sector, so at the end of the month he rented a room in a tenement, where he was not obliged to have contact with the neighbors. He also left the construction work and looked for another job.

1952—After taking up compulsory membership in the Perónist party he started work as layout designer for an official evening newspaper. There he met a draftsman who introduced him to an artistic circle, clearly anti-Perónist, since the general conviction was that "Perón uses the ignorant masses to attain power for himself." Two years later both were denounced because of this, and were dismissed. In the interim certain aspects of Leo's personal life had a stationary phase.

Stationary phase

From his experiences he had concluded that his least conflictual sexual enjoyment was achieved with prostitutes, whom he avoided seeing a second time. He preferred the distrust they showed on a first date while the lascivious eagerness they expressed in any subsequent encounter repulsed him. But this system had two disadvantages—it was expensive and it took time to constantly find new faces. Because of that Leo tried to reduce the meetings to one a week.

During a first stage he looked for women on Saturdays, but he soon discovered that on that day they were more sought-after and consequently the prices went up. Wednesdays were the easiest—he'd find them and bring them up to his room late; besides, that was a way of dividing his work week into two parts. He would look for them at railroad stations or around the waterfront bars. But those seven days passed slowly, he couldn't sleep nights, relentless erections kept him awake until his pride gave in and he masturbated, something which in his mind was only permissible in teenagers. He tried to avoid the habit, and to that end he began to jot down his masturbations in a notebook. He planned to skip two nights between one ejaculation and the next, but he couldn't. He settled for falling into temptation every other day—Fridays, Sundays, and Tuesdays—although he hated the aftereffect: the next morning he would unfailingly have headaches and depressions. On Sundays he'd stay in his room and the masturbation would begin as soon as he woke up, but when he'd feel the orgasm approaching he'd interrupt the act and go out for lunch, then he'd return and continue the act, prolonging it until four or five in the afternoon: the important thing was to ejaculate once, because two times produced decidedly unbearable migraine headaches. The process over, around six o'clock he'd meet a friend to go see a show or he'd go alone, retiring to bed before midnight. The alternatives were always the same, the movies or the theater. If he didn't have company for the evening he gave up the idea of going to the theater because it was humiliating to be alone in the intermissions, his greatest fear being that he would be spotted by some acquaintance.

On the other hand at the movies he could take the precaution of entering the theater when the lights were already out, and he could leave his seat a few minutes before the show was over; from the last row in the orchestra he would read the words The End. Being seen alone in a theater meant doom to Leo: he who didn't have company on Sundays had failed in life.

His eldest sister

On his first day of unemployment after being dismissed from the newspaper, Leo decided to visit Amalia, his eldest sister, in the hospital to which she had been admitted. He reached the second floor determined not to speak to the sick woman about his dismissal so as not to worry her. In the corridor the younger sister was crying in her husband's arms: Amalia, thirty-eight and single, was in danger of dying; the simple appendectomy had been complicated by an embolism. Leo went to the chapel of the hospital and prayed after many years of not doing so, he cried at length and asked that he die in Amalia's place; for the first time since the day the police tortured him he attained a total spiritual calm, a sensation of justice, already surrendering to death with all his heart. That night Amalia got over the supposedly fatal crisis and Leo felt somewhat annoyed by the good news. He was aware of the duality of his feelings and was ashamed of himself.

1955—After months of unemployment, Leo got a job as editor and graphics expert at an advertising agency. Again Olga had intervened with her influential friends. He was there when Perón's government fell. Leo felt an immense joy upon reflecting that those police torturers no longer had any power. But after a while he remembered the words of another man who had been detained—"I swear that the day Perón falls, and he's going to fall no matter how many fucking peasants defend him, that same day I'm going to come to this police station and do justice with my

93

own hands"—, and he felt sorry for the policemen, was determined to go himself to the police station and warn them of the danger they were in. A champagne celebration at the agency detained him.

New phase

A certain aspect of Leo's personal life, in the interim, had entered a new phase. A friend from the agency spoke to him about an elegant bar where at tea time one could meet lower- and upper-middle-class women—some of them married—favorably disposed to spending a pleasant moment in the company of a gentleman without monetary gain. The operation was carried out from table to table by means of glances; after a while they'd go outside separately and would finally meet on the sidewalk. Leo's success was immediate and continuous. He'd avoid a second encounter with excuses and if he saw any of his conquests after that, with a dry greeting he'd avoid further entanglement.

Europe, January 1956—The new Minister of Foreign Relations appointed by the so-called Freedom Revolution, on the basis of an important recommendation, appointed Leopoldo Druscovich as third secretary of the Argentine Embassy in a Scandinavian country, where he would perform his duties until 1962. At that time a transfer to South Africa, hardly desirable, forced him to resign his commission.

Thus from 1956 to 1962 he remained in Europe and two perhaps interrelated facts took on importance during that period. a) Leo was annoyed by the presence of an employee of the Embassy whose duty was to be his secretary. The young Scandinavian had a perfect knowledge of Spanish and good connections in cultural circles. But he was obviously homosexual and, since the arrival of his new boss, the subordinate had not been able to take his eyes off him. Leo tolerated the situation for some time, but two months of adulation were more than he could stand. He requested that the secretary be transferred to the consul's office, but as the employee refused he was fired. Leo once more found himself at fault. b) The following week, toward the end of the icy nordic winter, Leo caught pneumonia. After his stay in a hospital he then convalesced in his apartment, under the care of an old housekeeper. The doctor had prescribed rest, a lot of food, and total sexual abstinence. Leo obeyed every injunction. They were the happiest weeks of his life. In that furnished apartment which he rented there was a large collection of art books. Leo managed after some effort to concentrate on his reading and the hours passed quickly. In those weeks he read and studied all that he could find on the fine arts and he outlined a program of visits to European museums during weekends and vacations. Besides, recuperated by then, as a hygienic measure he decided to call upon the services of prostitutes who would perform fellatio on him, a sexual contact which did not cause any complications and which allowed him to maintain the clearheadedness necessary to fulfill his plan of study. But it must also be added that his sexual needs were less than those usual in him, since his enthusiasm for study absorbed many of his energies.

When six years later he finished his diplomatic mission, Leo returned to Argentina with a profound knowledge of the material studied.

Back from Europe

On the basis of his significant savings, the ex-official Leopoldo Druscovich opened an art gallery in Buenos Aires and shortly afterward sold it because the commercial side of the enterprise bored him. Besides, that way he could dedicate all his time to a magazine where he had charge of the section on fine arts. It was his first job as editor.

Marital status

Leo reached thirty-one years of age, now back in his country without ever having had a sexual relationship that was at the same time emotional. That is why, faced with the unaccustomed stability of his relations—which were intermittent, it is important to point out—with Miss Amalia Kart, the layout designer of the magazine, Leo decided to get married, hopeful of putting an end to his sexual disturbances. These consisted of the same upsetting accident as always: his erection would subside during intercourse and he would not reach orgasm.

A short time after his marriage, the accident—which had never occurred during months of sporadic premarital contact—occurred with his wife for the first time. The following week it was repeated and a month later the difficulty became chronic. At the beginning she cooperated patiently and tenderly, but the moment came when her nerves could not resist the test: it was morning, an opportune cold of Leo's had served as an excuse to cancel sexual encounters for several days, and when his wife tried to get up to put on her bathrobe Leo grabbed her brutally from behind making her fall on the bed. What then followed she would never forgive him for, because her evasive attitude unleashed insults, shoves, struggles, spitting, kicks, and a punch which broke her upper left canine tooth. Upon seeing the blood Leo stopped his assault and lay down on the bed panting. She dragged herself along the floor in the direction of the bathroom. He threatened her: "If you don't say what you're thinking this very moment I'll kick you in the stomach." She, on the floor, hesitated and then risked an answer: "Impotent, that's what you are, impotent." He wanted to carry out his threat to kick her but his arms and legs did not respond; he felt paralyzed by those words. His wife got dressed while he stared at the wires that went from the nightlamp and the fan to the socket. She left.

Her parents went to see her off at the Buenos Aires airport when, indemnified by the six thousand dollars Leo had been saving in the bank, she left for a long trip to Europe, where she settled.

After that unhappy event, Leo's sexual relations were totally discontinued. He returned to masturbation, as more secure ground, and only when the boredom of solitude prevented him from ejaculating would he resort to a prostitute for a relaxing fellatio, although by then that type of professional in Argentina, where they spoke Spanish like himself, was repulsive to him.

Leo's professional success

The work at the magazine absorbed his time, and the impact of his critiques grew. In 1966 an industrialist in search of good opportunities for investment suggested to him the founding of another magazine, similar to the one in which he had collaborated, but with more space devoted to art and entertainment. Leo accepted. When the 1968 season began the new publication was already recognized as the most important of its kind, and it was well known that for a production in the fields of art, music, theater, or literature its support was essential. To fully assume the responsibility that this prestige implied, Leo decided to initiate psychotherapeutic treatment, for the sake of the magazine rather than for his own benefit.

VII

Norma Shearer: (a young woman whose hair has turned white after a few months in the People's Prison, walks up the platform of the guillotine where she's to be decapitated, suddenly she remembers herself as an enraptured adolescent in the Viennese palace at the time of her prospective engagement to the Dauphin of France) I'll be queen of France! (the drums roll, the queen's head falls and the crowd roars with excitement)

The dashing young diplomat: (overlooking the savage spectacle from a tower, he lifts his eyes to the sky, then looks at the inscription in the ring that the beautiful Queen of France once gave him, reading it to himself) "Everything leads to thee."

(from *Marie Antoinette*, Metro-Goldwyn-Mayer)

Buenos Aires, April 1969

My nails, well-kept, not long, polished cyclamen pink, healthy and strong, they are filed but not sharp and the sheet's color is impossible to remember in the semi-darkness, it covers the designs on the mattress. Perhaps those designs represent plumes of imperial Roman helmets, shields and lances appearing among the thick foliage of

98

certain trees which also appear often in Gobelin tapestries, mattress fabrics with plumes, lances, shields, thick foliage, all in white and blue or white and pink are those fabrics for mattresses, my nails sink slowly into the sheet and push down the fabric which encloses bolts of combed wool. A wool tuft covers each of the stitches that are inserted between slight, even hills, for my nails to sink into? because the fabric yields but the nail's edge doesn't reach the point of cutting, it barely marks the sheet and blowing lightly over the palm of my hand the mouthful of air is warm like the wool and like the air between the two sheets. The thigh and knee run slowly along the sheet toward an edge of the bed which is next to the wall, they stop a moment and return to their place. The skin is somewhat cooler than the warm sheets, and from the skin moving inward the flesh that grows warmer and warmer from contact with the hot bones and the heating unit cannot be touched because it burns, and a proper diet of dairy products gives the organism the calcium it needs for strength. The radiator consists of a geometric net of pipes with hot water running through them, a screw and nut regulates the increasing or decreasing intake of water and through there a constant drop and a muffled sizzle escape, some horns and motor noises from the street traffic pierce the glass of the windows and putting the wristwatch against the ear one can perceive the tick-tack. Closing one's eyes it is also possible to hear a slight panting, no, at this moment the two bodies are at rest. The blood that circulates through his body, and also through mine, fulfills its course at an astonishing speed but in total silence, and at moments at even a greater speed, the heart beats faster than ever and the chest dilates so as not to press on it and to allow the silent—but not therefore cold—blood, at a temperature perhaps higher than that of the skin, to in turn dilate the heart, and already the only thing one can wish for is to rest, such a wave rises from the diaphragm that the filled lungs dislodge the well-earned yawn, the waistline fatigued from quietly pressing for a whole hour toward his vertical body. There are mirages in the desert, at the edge of this unusually wide bed if I close my eyes I don't see Leo Druscovich sleeping, but I hear—if a car in the traffic doesn't blow its horn—his almost imperceptible breathing. If I don't hear that either, without making the slightest noise I can sit up and from this end of the wide almost square bed I can move toward him and touch him. What if he wakes up? perhaps he will be annoyed because rest is necessary, closed eyes can't see anything. If he continues sleeping and keeps his eyes closed he won't see anything ugly, as if he were blind. What do people think of when they already have everything they want and cannot ask for anything more? The same as in heaven, they don't think of anything and they sleep, they rest, although it would be nice to think of something. What do the people in heaven think? only of nice things.

Interview that a lady reporter from the Parisian fashion magazine Elle *did of Gladys, according to the latter's imagination while resting beside sleeping Leo*

Reporter: To gain your absolute confidence—I know, you are quite shy—I will allow you to choose the name of this article.

Gladys: I wouldn't know what to say.

R: What do you think of "Gladys Hebe D'Onofrio Is in Heaven"?

G: I consider it a realistic title and to the point. But for your readers we should use a glamorous Hitchcockian language, "The Buenos Aires Affair" should be the title.

R: Because of your unprecedented talent you have become a star in the world of the arts in only a few months. Do you believe that you have now achieved your highest ambition?

G: No, my highest ambition is to fulfill myself as a woman in matters of love, and what a paradox, in my case my career has led me to love.

100

R: This is difficult to believe. Don't all career women say just the opposite?

G: Let them say it.

R: My intention is not to argue but to induce you to tell us, the readers of *Elle*, what a day in the life of the woman of the year is like.

G: I refuse, the most interesting minutes in the day of the life of the woman of the year are too ribald.

R: So that's how it is. Well then, if you don't want to tell us your story, begin by telling us the love story that you would have preferred to live.

G: Impossible. I consider my own love story unequaled.

R: Since you deny us entrance to your inner self, would you be willing to answer our mediocrity test?

G: Yes, I am willing, although in this moment what I'd most desire would be to spread on my skin the Polynesian body perfume that is recommended on a page in your magazine, because tonight I want to surprise someone with a new fragrance.

R: What led you to notice our suggestion about a better perfume?

G: The illustration of Polynesian girls, it shows them as fresh as the breeze from the surf, just as the rosebuds that fall upon the wet sand are soft, just as the flaming sunsets of the islands are warm. Pearl essence scent for the body.

R: Exactly. And now the first question: When you have to select a gift, do you tend to buy something that you yourself like, or rather, do you decide on something that the person in question *should* have?

G: I would buy something that I like.

R: Perfect! The supermediocre person would have bought something mentioned some time ago, and the mediocre one, something considered useful. Second question: If in the new fall season the Parisians decide to introduce as the latest fashion the helmet and armor of the Valkyries, would you be the first to put up with an outfit that weighs 25 pounds or would you run out to buy a classic Chanel tailleur or would you rather burst into resounding laughter?

G: I would burst into resounding laughter.

R: Perfect! Mediocrity is not your forte, Gladys Hebe D'Onofrio. Third and last question: If a young friend of yours—a girl fresh out of high school—asks your advice, would you tell her to enter the School of Architecture, travel to Biafra as a voluntary nurse, or set sail for India to study with the Maharishi?

G: Biafra.

R: What a pity. You're saved from the supermediocre, but you didn't choose the Maharishi, which is the fascinating and new thing to do.

G: My average isn't bad, right?

R: Very good.

G: And what do I care? What I do care about is that at eleven this morning iron knuckles knocked on my door. Before opening I asked who it was, thinking it was anybody but him . . . I met him a few months ago, at a beach where I was trying to recover my health, a nervous breakdown had undermined my constitution . . . One night I took a walk down by the sea, wearing the model labeled "water panther," bought in New York with close to a month's salary. There was nobody on the beach, water panther!, bathing suit and evening gown, all in one, black silk lit by acrylic teardrops. I prayed for someone to see me, looking more elegant than ever. The perfect tones of the night, the black of the water, the black of the sky, incandescent dots in the lampposts along the seaside promenade, incandescent dots in the crest of the black waves, in the acrylic drops, in the stars in the sky.

R: And that night you met him, the answer to your prayer.

G: No. That night I felt lonelier than ever. Imprisoned by despair I returned to the cottage and, almost crazed, I had an inspiration. I couldn't sleep. At five the dawn found me on the beach, for the first time picking up the debris that the surf had left on the sand. Flotsam, I only dared to love flotsam, anything else was too much to dare hope for. I returned home and began to talk—in a whisper so as not to wake up mama—with a discarded slipper, with a bathing cap in shreds, with a torn piece of newspaper, and I started to touch them and to listen to their voices. That was my work of art, to bring together scorned objects to share with them a moment of life, or life itself. That was my work. Between my last painting and this latest production more than ten years had passed. Now I knew why I hadn't painted or sculpted in all that time: because oils, temperas, water colors, pastels, clay, easels, all that was precious, expensive material I was not allowed to touch—an inferior being is not allowed to use up, waste, play with valuable objects. That's why for years I did nothing, until I discovered those poor fellow creatures who are rejected each morning by the tide . . .

R: Don't stop.

G: I don't know, it seems that all that followed was a dream, and that I am still as destitute as I was then.

R: Your reality today is different.

G: Yes, it's true . . . As I was saying, after that discovery I continued working, until one day the first group of vacationers came to the beach. I had heard that the men wore their hair very long and with them the women bathed bare-breasted. The windows of my makeshift work room faced a pine grove. On a tree branch a young man with a beard and very long hair was watching, listening to my conversation with the flotsam, judging my work. I closed the curtains. The following afternoon three men knocked on my door—they had very long hair—, accompanied by two women with—under blouses of fish net, gauze, crocheted straw—their breasts bare. Sometimes, after working the whole day, I'd close my eyes content with what I had done and I'd dare to think that people might see and hear my works and then praise them deliriously. I opened the door and the strangers came in, they asked to see and to listen. Those words of praise I had dreamed of in the solitude of White Beach now burst from the strangers' lips, but this is even more amazing; they repeated adjective for adjective, exactly, all that I had desired to hear. Sitting on my bench, a bench which before had been in the kitchen, and sitting on the floor around me, my first five friends asked me who I was and wondered why they had not met me before. They said that they would have liked to have created my works, and that afternoon we all went down to the sea together. Leo Druscovich, the only thing they regretted was that Leo Druscovich was not with us. Leo Druscovich, who is he?, and they all burst into the most good-natured laughter. "The Tsar of art criticism," nothing less, and in that way it became clear how foreign I was to the artistic movements in Argentina. Beach parties with an open fire till dawn, then happy dreams stretching to midday, there was only one thought that could keep me awake: two girls and three men invited me to stay with them in their tents at night, but they were so much younger than I. Almost two weeks of joy barely disturbed. They left.

R: Is it true that we women eat more when we feel sexually frustrated?

G: Yes, but at this moment I have a hard time remembering how a woman with sexual frustration feels.

R: In those moments of psychopathic gluttony, do you prefer sweets or salty foods?

G: I don't remember if it was in your magazine that I saw an advertisement for several Poitiers canned crêmes, served in crystal cups.

R: My magazine doesn't advertise fattening products. But I seem to remember a fine Baccarat cup with a short figured stem and a wide mouth, filled halfway with honey-colored crême topped with a bunch of cherries: as the finishing touch, a snowy peak of meringue.

G: And the other cup with a rough base is full of dark chocolate crême, with a simple star made of five peeled almonds on top. And the champagne glass contains four small peaches tinted red with angostura bitters and almost drowned in light yellow crême.

R: Different canned crêmes, chocolate, vanilla, praliné, mocha, caramel.

G: Also a crême with cordials in it, a recipe of some French monk.

R: Tell me more about Leo Druscovich.

G: Mama was playing canasta that afternoon, I was trying to resume my work again after my companions left. There was a knock on the door. Without ever having seen that man I already knew him: I had imagined him.

R: Why don't you dare say that you had dreamed of him?

G: Because I never have happy dreams, only nightmares. But in the wakefulness of more than one night I had . . . seen him, driving his sports car with the top down, to some nightclub on the bank of the River Plate, the pool reflecting the orchestra, an icy crystalline sea-green pool. He dances with a model who will hold his interest for only a few hours. And days later the wind blows stronger, Leo alone on the open pampas, a thick scarf protects his neck, and what is his windbreaker made of?, neither leather nor corduroy, it must be that rough army material, lined with goatskin. He gets out of the Land-Rover with a double-barreled gun, the smoke from the pipe warms his chest, he needs to escape his urban problems for a few hours, hunting partridges, he has to kill in order to amuse himself. I'll never understand men, and you? do you by any chance understand the pleasure they get from watching boxing? Have you seen the joy on their expectant faces when the boxer's features have been completely transformed into a shapeless mass?

R: That means that men are not afraid of pain as we are, they don't get intimidated so easily, because in the face of danger a real man becomes . . . bigger.

G: Are you sure of that?

R: Please don't stop, continue with your story.

G: Where was I? Ah yes, after having sentenced himself to solitude and the pampa winds for hours, he returns to the city, running away from a neurotic and possessive woman, the wife of his best friend, a ranchowner. He should have spent the weekend with them, but already the horses have to be hitched to the carriage to take Leo to the not very distant railroad station. And the train moves through the pampas, Leo returns to his prison of cement, traffic, incessant traffic lights and vanity: the capital of the Argentine Republic, Santa María de los Buenos Aires, those Good Airs filled with homicidal gases. Leo, loved by too many women and envied by too many men . . . Thus did I imagine your days and nights, until you entered my life. But it was Saturday, and our hero will dedicate the remaining day of rest—enclosed in his library—to the study of the great figures of the history of art, his great white passion.

R: White passions. Are there purple ones?

G: Yes, the man who likes to make people suffer is excited by rooms without windows, strangled faces are purple. Didn't you know?

R: I'm beginning to understand you, Gladys Hebe D'Onofrio, to such a point that when one day he knocked on your door I know how you would have liked to be attired: simple reminiscences of a Dresden shepherdess, whose lace is no longer wrought in china, the transparent organdy reveals a tanned, golden complexion. Transparent wiles of organdy.

G: Only comparable to the formidable guiles of lace . . . Yes it's true, because the attire chosen was white like a camellia.

R: Its fringes, on the other hand, were soaked in almost orange tints.

G: Up until this point you're right. Continue.

R: Proudly free of jewels.

G: Wrong, I would have been ostentatiously covered with them. I opened the door and invited him in.

R: The door of this hotel room?

G: The door of the White Beach cottage. His friends had told him about me and he had come there especially to meet me. Barely looking at me, he asked to see my works. He saw them and heard them, said that I was his choice for representing the country at the next Exhibition in São Paulo. Only then did he look at me fully to catch my predictable Cinderella reaction. I did not outwardly show the slightest emotion, it was not at all difficult to restrain myself, because São Paulo had no importance whatsoever after seeing such a man enter my door. All that mattered after having seen him was to spend the rest of my life near him to be able to look at him. But here's where the conflict comes in, because I can only see Leo in his totality when he looks at me.

R: What is the look of Leo Druscovich like?

G: I don't know, a cyclone sweeps me off the earth and carries me to unknown territories, where I am caught by rays that read one's thoughts, or electrify, or kill, or give life. I don't know.

R: Tell me, I must find out.

G: The peerless critic thought that I was an impassive, dedicated artist, deaf to the flatteries of fortune and he felt that this doubled his admiration for my works.

R: Repeat to me the words of the critic.

G: "Perhaps you didn't hear me well: I am chairman of the committee that selects the works to be presented at São Paulo and I've just designated you as the official representative of Argentina." I—impassive, with only time to observe how the waves of his hair caressed his bull-like neck—answered that I had heard him the first time. He added: "I don't understand you. Why don't you jump with joy? Why don't you shout?" I looked at his hands to see if he wore an engagement ring, he didn't have one. Thinking that this man—cultured, powerful, master of my artistic destiny, handsome, temperamental, neurotic, mysterious—was still waiting for the ideal companion, thinking about all that distracted me and I didn't hear what he was saying and I didn't answer him.

He became annoyed. "I repeat, why aren't you interested in such an opportunity? The only possible justification would be your desire to work, and not interrupt your creativity." I had a ready answer: "Yes, that's the reason, I'm working well and I don't want interruptions for the moment." He turned around and disappeared. The slamming of the door made us, me and my works, tremble. As is to be expected, that night I couldn't sleep and dawn had not yet arrived when I went down to the beach in search of garbage for the making of new works. Far out in the ocean the dying lights of fishing boats, on the wet sand rusty tin cans, on the dunes a shadow and a red signal of alarm: a lighted cigarette. I trembled with fear, the shadow moved. It was coming in my direction. Who could be on the beach at that hour but a madman, a lunatic? In my hand was a sharp pebble I had recently picked up, my only weapon. It would have been senseless to run. I began to tremble, I had lost control of my body, the shadow stopped, the light-colored pants were profiled in the distance, the torso was wrapped in a darker material that did not succeed in hiding the brutal strength of bulky muscles. The pebble fell from my trembling hand. Mutely I prayed that this man would let me escape, or that someone would come by on the coastal highway. I looked north and south, the two *sfumato* limits of the highway, not a single vehicle in sight . . . A strong man needs only his hands to destroy a woman's weak neck, under the pressure of those claws the bones break like cartilage, the skin tears like paper. Master of the dying female body, that monster with the deformed face—his eyes are mere slits bordered by giant warts—can bring his slimy skin close to hers, and she's already dead from repugnance . . . All that passed through my mind like dark lightning and the new morning from one moment to the next gave off an almost day-like light. The burning cigarette became less brilliant, the shadow acquired the forms and colors of Leo Druscovich. Strong forms, friendly colors.

R: Like those Nice landscapes of the good Matisse?

G: Translucid, soaked in white. "Can you carry that load back to your house alone? Here, let me help you." During the walk we spoke of the good weather we were having on the coast, at my door he remained silent for a moment; for fear of the ridiculous way my mother might react, I didn't mention the possibility of his coming in for a hot drink. He stopped looking directly at me. Like a little boy scolded for some mischief, his eyes suddenly became sad and evasive. He took leave of me, making a date to have dinner together that very night. I went to bed without taking all that I had gathered on the beach out of the bag. One question kept pressing me: what had he been doing on the beach at that hour? At the end of a short nap I woke up, tense, and in vain tried to get back to sleep. The cause of my insomnia this time couldn't have been more frivolous: for the date that night I literally didn't have anything to wear. I would have loved to appear radiant with luxury.

R: And what for you is luxury?

G: My idea of luxury among other things means sleeping until noon, wrapped in the linen of light, fine, soft, and fresh sheets. Every day, fresh newly perfumed sheets.

R: Perfumed?

G: Yes, on a meadow sheets are spread out in the sun which warms them. When they're brought back inside they again take on room temperature, but the heat doesn't leave, it turns into sun perfume.

R: Hmm . . . How did you dress that night?

G: We ate lobster, white wine is the color of amber, so why do they call it that. When I was a little girl, my secret desire was to catch fire in my hand, the little red translucid flames that hot coals give off are fascinating.

R: And the green flames with yellow tips from kerosene heaters?

109

G: And the little blue tongues, each the same size, on a gas stove? Liquid amber-colored fire in my glass, that night I wanted to inject fire into myself drinking it as he did, but I couldn't because I'd taken barbiturates before we met. I'm scared of dying one day because of carelessness with drugs.

R: Alcohol and barbiturates, the traffic lights have turned red.

G: The day that preceded that dinner was very long, I consumed a double, a triple dose of tranquilizers. When I reached the restaurant my eyes were almost closed in sleep. He immediately asked me why I looked so tired. I answered that I had spent the whole day creating. I asked him to tell me what his life was like in Buenos Aires, that city I didn't understand. He drank wine, ate very little, and talked, about his projects, about the importance of the Argentine artistic movement. I felt that my eyes were closing, I tried to pay attention to what Leo was saying but besides the fact that my eyelids were heavy, I was hypnotized by his mouth, by his mustache that moved to and fro, the mustache stretched and returned to its place, and his eyes nailed me against the stately high-backed chair, in that large Renaissance dining room.

R: Tell me something about the mouth of that man.

G: I can't avoid the cliché: his mouth is sensual.

R: And you were soon asleep.

G: Exactly. While he spoke and looked at me I managed to keep my eyes open, but the moment that he lowered his eyes to prepare a cigar and light it was fatal for me.

R: Who woke you up?

G: The maître. Leo had paid and gone. There was nobody left in the restaurant. A dishwasher came in from the kitchen with a pail of water to put out the flame on the salamander stove.

R: Who took you home?

G: Several days later I received a special delivery letter from Buenos Aires. Without mentioning the incident at

110

the restaurant at all, he asked me if a trip to Buenos
Aires to discuss my presentation at São Paulo would fit
into my immediate plans. But don't you think that our
indiscreet conversation might wake Leo up?

R: Let's speak in a whisper.

G: I wrote to him about my approaching trip to Buenos
Aires, without giving a date. Already settled in this
hotel, with all my materials carefully put away in
storage, I called him on the telephone. Twenty minutes
later, someone who had escaped the doorman's watchful
eye was knocking on my door. I opened, I was so excited I couldn't speak. All that happened yesterday.

R: How were you dressed?

G: I had just washed my hair, the white towel wrapped
like a turban hiding my hair. And that bathrobe which
you can now see thrown on the floor, yellow terrycloth, a
color which goes well with a tan.

R: And your famous dark glasses, I presume.

G: Neither of us uttered a word. Finally he said: "Let me
come in, if they see me in the hallway they'll throw me
out." He came in. He embraced me. He kissed me. We
continued standing in the room silently kissing several
minutes more, we couldn't tear away from each other.
Already exhausted by the excitement and joy I withdrew
my mouth and leaned my forehead on his shoulder. The
turban came undone and fell to the floor. He tried to kiss
me again. I kept moving my face away. He sought my
mouth. I resisted. He became inflamed with passion. I
struggled to free myself. He imprisoned my hands in his
big hands, he bent my arms against my back and held
me tighter than ever against him. His strength was much
greater but I continued struggling. He began to kiss my
neck and with his snout parted my bathrobe until he
uncovered a shoulder, from there down to my breast.
Suddenly his strength tripled, he lifted me in the air and
deposited me on the bed. I was exhausted, but didn't
know how to give in with dignity. I lay still. He took off
his jacket and began to undo his tie, without taking his

111

eyes off me. **He** was so handsome. I closed my eyes to engrave in my memory that look of desire. And I didn't dare open them again. I heard his footsteps going toward the window, the sound of the Venetian blinds falling, his footsteps coming near. When I opened my eyes, his were staring at me, he tried to take off my dark glasses, I begged him not to, he took off my robe, he had a hard time undoing the inside button of the belt. He kissed me, spread my legs, and caressed my most intimate parts . . . When one tries to take hold of burning red logs sputtering gold sparks, when one tries to catch the highest and most vibrant flame of a bonfire, the pain of the wounds is so great that forgetting all that colorful splendor we flee screaming. But if one is a prisoner, entangled in the bush, held down by those two strong oak branches, or arms? which stop us, all that's left is to wait for the flesh to burn until it is consumed . . .

R: But why do you stop? What are you thinking of?

G: I remembered something curious. In his arms I thought that if he was so handsome it was thanks to me, who had known how to draw him to perfection at the "Leonardo da Vinci" Institute.

R: Continue.

G: He asked me if I loved him. I was afraid of telling him the truth, that I had adored him since the first moment I saw him. I preferred to say nothing. He smoked a cigarette in silence. He got dressed and left.

R: And today he came back again.

G: When the banging of iron knuckles could be heard I trembled from head to toe.

R: Of course, but first tell me what you did between yesterday and today.

G: I slept many hours, waking up from one moment to the next with the impression that he was in the room and might become bored if I didn't talk to him or show him something interesting. And besides sleeping I spent a few hours in the bathtub. And this morning I went to the hairdresser.

R: Was your sexual encounter today less or more intense than yesterday's?

G: When I was in San Francisco it was hard for me to believe that such a stately modern city was built on the ruins and panic of an earthquake.

R: This last question will be difficult for me to put to you as easily as it will be for you to answer. How should I phrase it? . . . A man, when walking on the street, or when in a living room, or in the most intimate conversation, gives an image of himself, which at times does not coincide with the other image of the flesh projected through the total contact of the boudoir.

G: I understand.

R: You better. Does the mental image you had of Leo harmonize or clash with the image of Leo in the flesh?

G: I opened the door and he came in without looking me in the eyes. I asked him if he would have a cup of tea with me. As you can see, in this comfortable hotel each room comes equipped with a cute kitchenette. And guess what, he said yes, and handed me the umbrella and raincoat that I asked for. He inquired if I wanted to go out, to see some exhibition, or some movie. I answered him—with my back turned, busy preparing the tea—that there was nothing that interested me in particular. When I turned around I saw that he was already almost naked in the middle of the room, his pants, jacket, shoes and vest thrown on the floor. He was unknotting his tie. Such insolence offended me and I ordered him to get dressed immediately. He laughed and took off his jock shorts. I couldn't take my eyes away in time and I saw his stiff phallus, in daylight his dimensions frightened me, I thought of my organs still impaired by the attack the day before, I thought of an illustration in my third or fourth grade reader with pictures of dungeons, stocks, racks, the instruments of torture with which the Spaniards martyrized the old Argentine patriots of 1810. He threw himself upon me and began kissing me by force. I didn't dare scream for help to the hotel servants.

113

But I continued to refuse him—no man can respect a woman who lets herself be taken by force!, I concluded in my heart of hearts—and I continued fighting until my arms lost their strength. Until then my refusal was of a moral order, my own imposition, but when I felt him dripping sweat I was truly revolted. This last convulsive shuddering found my body without defenses, the tears flowed and I began to shake like a dead leaf swept by the wind. His hands firmly spread my legs, I begged him in an almost unintelligible murmur not to do it. The rest I remember only vaguely, perhaps it was the fear of suffering that caused me to faint, I only know that when I recovered consciousness and felt him moving rhythmically inside me, I could barely find my own hands—hanging lifelessly over the sides of the bed as if crucified—to hold onto his back, the skin of his back was damp, I felt for a tip of the sheet and dried it. He kissed me tenderly. Our mouths could no longer be separated. I waited for him to be the first to withdraw his lips to then tell him yes, I love him, as he had asked me the afternoon before. But I couldn't utter a word, the pleasure started to climb from my belly to my throat. I opened my eyes, saw his eyelashes, his temple, a lock of dark blond hair.

R: What did you think of in that climactic moment?

G: I didn't think of anything.

R: According to the latest psychoanalytical theories people who make love without thinking about anything can consider themselves healthy.

G: Then I'm not a healthy woman, because now I remember that when pleasure forced me with its silky, strangling hand to close my eyes again, I thought that heaven existed. That God loved me and that's why he had rewarded me after so much suffering, with a true love. God asked me if I was ready for any sacrifice for the love of my future companion. I answered that of course I was, what's more, it would be my pleasure to bend under Leo's will.

114

R: Do you remember the dress you had on at that moment? In heaven, I mean.

G: I believe I was wearing the water panther outfit, but I couldn't swear to it.

R: Don't you think that we women are braver than we think? Think of what it means to lock oneself in a room with a being three times our strength.

G: Strength that he needs to protect his beloved. What would become of us if in the middle of the jungle his strong arm did not deal the fatal ax blow upon the crouching leopard?

R: Do you have anything else to tell me before I take leave of you?

G: Yes, that when he wakes up I will tell him . . . that I love him, that from now on his will shall be mine. Up until now he has judged me as cold and proud, and that's why he thought so much impetus was necessary. When he knows me as I am, he will love me even more.

R: He is stirring. Have we awakened him with our conversation? I'm going . . .

G: Before you go I want to ask you a question. When will the article you announced in your magazine on the so-called roots of feminine beauty, appear?

R: I've seen the advertisement, but that rot won't appear in my magazine.

G. I was charmed by the way the advertisement approached the problem: "Does your beauty have instinctual or cerebral roots? An existential, physical, or wardrobe origin? Where does it really stem from? Find out." I want to know, because ever since I've been feeling beautiful I've been goaded by curiosity, am I an instinctual or an existential beauty?

VIII

The thief: (hidden from the police for years in the winding paths of the Casbah) So you decided to come back here, and take another look at the beast . . . What do you think of my cage? What do you think of the Casbah?

Hedy Lamarr: I don't like to travel, it makes me homesick. When I wake up and I don't see Paris, I'd rather close my eyes again. Do you know Paris?

The thief: (proudly) Every street, every alley, every boulevard . . .

Hedy Lamarr: (looking at the miserable tavern in which they have met) We're a long way from home.

The thief: (pointing to the jewels she's wearing) Places like this . . . don't make you uneasy?

Hedy Lamarr: Not if I'm with you, Pepe LeMoko.

The thief: (holding her in his arms) You're beautiful! But that's easy to say . . . You must be tired of hearing it. What I want to express is different. For me you're more than beautiful. For two years I've been lost, like walking in my sleep. Suddenly I wake up— that's you—and I don't know how I went on all that time waiting for you. You know what you are to me? Paris! That's you . . . The whole town!

Hedy Lamarr: (tenderly) It's time to go. I'll try to come back tomorrow. Early. But . . . in case it's impossible for me, couldn't you get out of the Casbah to meet me, Pepe?

(from *Algiers*, United Artists)

CURRICULUM VITAE

(an application which the artist María Esther Vila picked up to present to the Organizing Committee of the International Exhibition, to take place at São Paulo during the month of July 1969).

Name:
Place and date of birth:
Marital status:
Residence:
Studies:
Artistic achievements:
Awards:
Statement of proposed project for the São Paulo Exhibition:
Date of presentation of the present report:

Leopoldo Druscovich's words during a visit to his doctor, April 24, 1969

. . . in the dream I was here and you were showing me those illustrations with printed ink blots, which they used to do tests with, they were symmetrical, remember? And in the dream they were all butterflies, none of them intact, they all had some defect, and of course, the defects repeated on both sides, because those ink blots are symmetrical. The wings were always broken. And I was looking for the butterfly that had only one broken wing. And there was no way to find it but you got angry. And suddenly the dream jumped to my office, and the boss was calling me and I was drawing a butterfly, but I had begun with the body and the boss called me and

117

I had to stop and there was only that body that without wings looks like an earthworm, a little boy's penis, gnawed at. And that's all. The boss was calling me . . .

. . . no, we haven't had an argument for a while . . . Well, just this week to be exact. But it wasn't an argument . . .

. . . I was finishing a very important article on primitive painting and he called me up. I answered that I couldn't go because I was busy, wasn't I right? I'm at the service of the firm and not of the owner. Interrupting the work at that moment could damage the article . . . because I felt really inspired at the moment. But, when I hung up and tried to continue working on the article I couldn't, I was tense, nervous. Whenever I have to defend myself I feel bad afterwards, does that happen to everybody or am I sick?

. . . this is nonsense . . . but what would happen if we went around naked in the office, yes, if the director saw that I have a penis he doesn't have. I've already explained it to you, I have an unusually large penis . . . so what would happen then?, would I rest easier by showing him my superiority? I don't know what would happen . . . because I am superior to him physically and in my capacity for work, but the two superiorities are concealed, one by clothes, and the other because he's the owner and I'm just the editor of a section of the magazine. And the magazine becomes a microcosm, right? where one takes for granted that the boss is superior to the rest . . .

. . . the butterflies were repulsive, I think. Once, some time ago, I had a nightmare about a bat, I remember, but it was a long time ago. But I don't remember what was going on, only that I felt a strong revulsion . . .

. . . yes, for me it's a disgusting bird, but it always attracted my attention. Now that I think of it the repulsive part is the body, because the wings have character, like the wings of the devil, that are copied from the bat. And of course, that's what makes it more disgusting: you look at it because of the wings that attract you, and then you discover that it's a rat, which like all rats is always in filth and you get angry at having looked at a sickening creature, which should be exterminated . . . They're blind during the day, they sleep like vampires. And their wings are used to beat the victim, when they fly they flutter their wings forcefully and big wings should be used to fly high and not to attack, the bat is an abortion of nature, that's what it is. It's an imperfect, monstrous being, it should be exterminated . . .

. . . yes, my eyes are closed, but nothing comes to mind now . . .

. . . a soldier in a hospital bed, his head completely bandaged, only his eyes are uncovered, like a mummy. It's a photograph I saw at the office today, of a soldier in the Mid-East, burned alive, but he's going to be okay . . .

. . . neither his father nor mother can go see him, I think they died in a bombardment. But he has visitors, charity ladies . . .

. . . the oldest one stands in front of my bed. She's from the Salvation Army. No, she's neither very old nor young, she asks me if I want something. I ask her to sing. She asks me what. I ask her for something they sing to the soldiers when they entertain on the battlefield. I think she's English, she sings to me with a British accent what they always sing to the soldiers. There's a song that I don't remember how it went . . . (he opens his eyes)

. . . no, in Tunisia, in Libya, during the Second World War, English and American actresses went, to sing to the soldiers . . .

. . . no, are you kidding, "Lili Marlene" is a gross commonplace. You underestimate me when you say that, see, in that sense you're conditioned by your limited artistic information, and you can't understand me . . .

. . . I'm not interested in discussing that with you, what I want is to remember that song, there was an American magazine during the war called *En Guardia*, it was free, North American propaganda you know, and I think it sometimes had songs for piano, and at home they would sing . . .

. . . no, they wouldn't sing "Lili Marlene" . . .

. . . with my little sister at the piano . . .

. . . she didn't like it either. It's not right for you to insist on irritating me, I have to make an effort to . . . control myself. Please don't irritate me . . .

. . . yes . . . let me think . . . Me and my sisters sang "Lili Marlene," I was little, in short pants. But then everybody began to sing it and we got tired of hearing it so much . . .

. . . yes, I have to admit, that's not very democratic, but it irritates me when something I like a lot becomes popular . . .

. . . I don't remember . . .

. . . when I was little, things like "Lili Marlene." From that you can get an idea . . . Later when I put on long pants it bothered me that Toulouse-Lautrec became popular, because the Americans made a movie about his life (he closes his eyes). And it scares me that a beautiful thing can one day become tiring. That means that you can't be sure of anything. Not even of the masterpiece kept in a museum. One moment . . . now I remember the song that the woman sang in the hospital, and she's a great lady, but in order to get the soldiers to be more affectionate with her . . . , or rather more trustful . . .

. . . yes, affectionate, why not . . . They feel affection for her almost as soon as they see her come in the ward. But they're a little afraid that she might be one of those cold, dried-out aristocratic ladies. But she takes off her hat, no, she's not wearing a hat, the Queen of England just passed through my mind, the mother of the present queen, but no, she doesn't look like the Queen of England, who does she look like? as soon as she comes in they all realize that she's a very good woman, a little old to be their girlfriend, and too young to be their mother . . . it's hard to explain . . . The beds are hospital beds, with iron bars painted white, and she holds on to the front bars of the bed of the sickest one of all, and she sings in a soprano voice, the words say that beyond the dark horizon hides the new dawn. Her eyes gaze at infinity. It's one of the loveliest songs there is . . .

. . . I don't think so, she succeeds in making him smile for the last time. The thought that the poor boy has before dying is that a new day is about to begin. She finishes the song and when she realizes he has died with his eyes open she lowers his eyelids, with all the delicacy she's capable of . . . At this moment I want her hand to lower my eyelids as well . . .

. . . and I want her to caress me, I am bandaged all over, only my eyes can be seen, I want her to caress my forehead . . .

. . . I have died, before seeing her come near, I barely managed to feel the soft, warm hand through the bandage. Her fingertips. And my face immediately turns cold, and is going to dry up, and crack, like ashes . . .

(he opens his eyes) . . . today I read that in the province of Santa Fe and part of Córdoba the drought is getting worse, and if it doesn't rain soon they're going to lose the crop, and that made me glad . . . The dry earth is going to split, and the wind begins to disintegrate it like sand and it flies, until there's nothing left but the rocky foundation, all stone. And that news made me happy . . .

. . . I don't wish anybody death, but suffering yes, I did wish suffering on somebody . . .

(he closes his eyes again) . . . I don't know what happens when the stone is exposed

121

. . . I would like to cry, the whole afternoon, not move from here and cry . . .

. . . no. Not for myself. Not crying for myself. I'm sure of that . . .

. . . for that dead soldier . . .

. . . not me. But someone took it upon himself to kill him . . .

. . . no. No friend of mine has died . . .

. . . no. Nobody in my generation . . .

. . . yes. I hurt somebody, and afterwards I was sorry . . .

(he opens his eyes) . . . once . . . I injured a boy, I didn't mean to . . .

. . . no, . . . with a brick . . .

. . . it was an accident, playing, I threw the brick in the air, I didn't think that he was so close . . . and he was there, . . . and I injured him on the nape of the neck . . .

. . . yes. They accused me of doing it on purpose . . . No, it's not true, nobody accused me . . .

. . . I never saw him again . . .

. . . nobody special, he was a friend, like the others. Or rather an acquaintance . . . (he sits up) I think I'm going to select the woman I sleep with as representative for the Exhibition . . .

. . . no, because I don't want to be corrupt, like other juries. Until I'm sure that I'm selecting her because she's really good I'm not going to decide . . .

. . . other opinions. First of all I got the opinion of friends, whom I respect. They made me go see her works. Perhaps they influenced me, that's what I don't know. I got to know the artist and her works at the same time . . . Although she's part of the work too, because she talks to her objects. That's her work, the relationship between her and her junk . . .

. . . what do I care what they think! What matters is what I think! . . .

(he doesn't obey, he keeps his eyes open) . . . Suddenly I put the light on to see the eye she always covers . . .

. . . at that moment I held her down, she couldn't move . . .

. . . because I don't like people to hide things from me . . .

. . . and I was nervous because of problems at the magazine. And that's all . . .

(silence, he walks around the room, he looks at the doctor) . . . sometimes it feels cold in this room. It's like a cell, with the curtains drawn (he lies down on the couch and closes his eyes). I think I'm going to spend my life with my eyes closed, that's the best thing there is . . . Now I remember the tune of that song . . .

. . . the one from the Second World War, that says that beyond the blue horizon hides the sun, but not at sunset, it says that it is night and the sky is blue but in reality night is black, right?, it says . . . beyond the blue horizon, and that the sun will come out soon although it's still completely dark out, it's what the charity lady sings to the dying soldier, I must have seen it in some movie, who knows how many years ago, and she might be dead now too, the war was twenty-four years ago, when my sister played that piece, and the older one turned the page and I . . . what did I do? what exactly did I do? . . .

. . . I wore short pants (he frowns, his eyes are still closed) I can't see anything . . . I can't imagine anything . . .

. . . I can't see anything,

only the edge of those white coral plants, on the bottom of the sea, they're like cartilage, I feel like touching them, to see if they're rough, if they scratch, they seem like lace, soft lace on old-fashioned underwear, they're plants, no, they're stones . . . if I bite the branch of a plant a liquid comes out, like a very sweet juice, there's something that runs like water inside a plant, if I'm dying of thirst I can chew it, even if it's a mere drop, but a stone doesn't give me anything, I sink my teeth into it and my teeth break. There are stone plants, I saw them somewhere, in fossil stones the leaves remain imprinted, it's night, . . . I'm in my bed . . . and sometimes I reach out and touch a sharp stone, it's dry, I begin to rub it and dust, sand comes off it, in the desert, if the wind rises the sand is going to fly and get in my eyes, I have to be careful not to rub the stones anymore because they're becoming sand, at the end of the horizon black air is rising, the black wind blew toward me so fast that sand got in my eyes, I didn't have time to close them, before the sand began to blow . . . but when mama died she was inside a house, a hospital with the windows closed so that sand wouldn't get in her eyes, in an oxygen tent they told me, no, papa died in an oxygen tent, but I didn't see him, my older sister went to Mendoza and saw him. But I didn't, I couldn't hug him before he died . . .

(after a long pause) . . . I have to decide the vote, help me . . .

. . . I don't know . . . they lack substance, a theoretical, conscious approach. And besides now another candidate has come up, there's more clarity in the things she does. While the other one doesn't know why she does them, and it's even possible that she hit on it by chance . . .

. . . no, I'm not contradicting myself, I told you that the artist must let himself be led by his darkest intuitions in order to create something new. But . . . it's difficult to explain, . . . the only thing that's certain is that all she's interested in is the Exhibition . . . (he stops)

. . . it's a very crude slang

expression, I'm disgusted by certain slang expressions, but it comes to my mind . . .

. . . that a cunt hair has more pull than a yoke of oxen . . .

. . . she began to disgust me . . .

. . . she began to disgust me. Because in her own way, timidly, she tries to manipulate me. Now I'm disgusted by her . . .

. . . I don't know . . . the second time we slept together I thought all the problems had ended . . . and for the first time I managed to do something that I had never been able to do: after everything came out well, I . . . slept with her in my arms, me who if I'm not alone in my own bed I can never fall asleep . . .

. . . when I woke up? I don't know . . . she began to be sweet to me . . . I sensed it in her voice that she wasn't sincere, that she was pretending. She got up to get things for me, to eat, things from outside, to fawn on me, I felt that a slimy slug was crawling over my body. Because she began to fawn on me . . . to make sure she got the prize . . .

. . . many things happened . . .

. . . I found her more and more disgusting . . .

. . . she's a hypocrite . . .

. . . yesterday I turned on the light . . . and I opened that eyelid that's closed with nothing inside . . . and I told her so, that . . . it's not my fault . . .

. . . no, when that begins . . . nothing can help . . .

. . . I don't want to have anything more to do with her . . . I've lied to you. The jury already chose the candidate. I voted for her. And she won. She's the one chosen for São Paulo . . .

. . . when that begins nothing can help . . . And the last time I couldn't. I already told you how it is. I can't ejaculate! First it seems like a passing thing, but then it's repeated . . .

. . . it's her fault, she's a bat . . . I told her so and she didn't say anything, if she said something I would have knocked her brains out . . .

(he obeys and closes his eyes again) . . . no, I don't see anything, I'm not thinking of anything but the siren of that fire engine on the street at this moment, or of an ambulance, I don't know what it is . . .

. . . they're taking me, I'm about to die . . .

. . . no, I'm alone . . .

. . . why? I want to die alone, I don't want anybody with me in that ambulance . . .

. . . I don't know why . . .

. . . I don't know. I don't know if I deserve it or not . . .

. . . if she was critically ill in the ambulance, and not me? . . .

. . . yes, she's going, she's about to die . . .

. . . yes, I feel sorry for her and I accompany her in the ambulance . . .

. . . she dies before the ambulance reaches the hospital. I'm looking at her and she dies. I'm holding her cold hand, she can no longer pull it away or defend herself, if I want I can take advantage of her. I don't know if the dead bleed. If one cuts the flesh of the dead with a surgical knife, opening a long, deep cut, I don't know if blood would come out . . .

. . . I feel like crying . . .

. . . I feel like crying because she died, and she wasn't to blame for anything . . .

. . . I feel very sorry . . .

. . . now that she's dead I

feel sorry, if I had known that she was going to die I would have told her that I love her, anything, so that she'd die in peace . . .

                              . . . it was my fault she died . . .

                         . . . she's dead . . . I slept at her side. That had never happened to me . . .

From the doctor's office Leopoldo Druscovich went directly home, he wanted to be alone. As usual, the evening newspaper was under the door. A news item cornered his attention: the corpse of a man had been found in a vacant lot on the outskirts of Buenos Aires. Missing for two weeks, the man's tragic end had been feared because of his subversive political activities. He was linked to an activist group that was fighting for the return of ex-president Perón to the country as the only means of giving the government back to the working class majority. The body had been abandoned in some bushes and showed signs of torture.

Part Two

IX

Nurse: (handing a glass of whiskey to her patient, a future alcoholic) Listen honey, I want you to take a sip, it's not the most suitable thing to do but it'll make you see things a little better.

Susan Hayward: (inconsolable since the death of her fiancé) No, thanks.

Nurse: Drink it, drink it in one gulp if you don't like it.

Susan Hayward: Why should I drink it?

Nurse: (with good intentions) It will make you sleep all night.

Susan Hayward: I don't like alcohol.

Nurse: It's good, it helps you forget.

Susan Hayward: Forget? What is it I should forget? David's love? his smile? his understanding? Don't you realize that I'm already forgetting, and that's what's killing me? Sometimes two, three days go by . . . and I can't remember his face! (losing control of her nerves) And you want to help me forget!!! (hysterically) What kind of person are you??!! (she sobs burying her head in the pillow, little by little she calms down) Excuse me, it's just that I'm feeling so bad, so confused . . . sometimes at night I wake up and I can't believe that it's at all true, I think that he never died, that everything has been a nightmare, that it can't be possible that the only good thing that's happened to me in my whole life is finished forever, . . . but I reach out my hand to touch him and there's nothing in the darkness . . . I touch nothing, and that nothing isn't him, that nothing is me . . . (the nurse brings the glass near the patient's lips, and the latter drinks the whole contents with effort)

(from *I'll Cry Tomorrow*, Metro-Goldwyn-Mayer)

Recapitulation—The reading of the newspaper item disturbed Leopoldo Druscovich, who during his insomnia decided, first, to approach the family of the dead man to offer them the only thing he could give, economic help, and secondly, to summon the artist who had emerged as a finalist—after the winner Gladys Hebe D'Onofrio—in the competition to represent Argentina at the São Paulo Exhibition. In the first as in the second case he was attempting to make amends for an injustice.

The next morning in the offices of the magazine everybody was talking about the crime in the vacant lot. Leo heard almost everyone agree that the activist's death was due to tortures inflicted in police headquarters, after which the authorities must have rid themselves of the corpse.

Hours later, as representative of his magazine, Leo gained access to the residence of the departed. The widow thanked him for his offer of money but rejected it, promising to keep that resource in mind in case of extreme need.

Leopoldo Druscovich's editorial office, April 22, 1969

Leopoldo Druscovich: What I find most striking about your works is their solidity, as if they were supported by a certain theoretical approach . . . which leaves no place for vagueness.

132

María Esther Vila:

LD: That is, you would not make a single brushstroke nor outline a single volume without knowing why you do it?

MEV:

LD: That is, a deliberate, conscious approach.

MEV:

LD: I don't understand.

MEV:

LD: What? The artist "existentially" implies that his approach is original?, what's that?

MEV:

LD: Original to and deliberately preceding the work?

MEV:

LD: Existentially? . . . But when you're working—I've read that other, very famous artists have said this—, don't you feel that you are carried away by a mysterious force that dictates things to you which you don't clearly know where they're taking you?

MEV:

LD: What? . . . That is, you don't believe in the unconscious as the prime mover of artistic creation.

MEV:

LD: Anyway . . . all this has to do with your being here today. You already know of course that the candidate for São Paulo has been chosen, but just the same . . . It is a matter that demands the greatest discretion.

MEV:

LD: The jury was a bit hasty perhaps . . . it has already chosen Gladys D'Onofrio as the Argentine representative, as you know. Well, the thing is I've begun to have my doubts . . . especially after talking to her a lot and noticing a total lack of what we were talking about . . . a theoretical, conscious approach.

The same office, April 27, 1969

MEV:

LD: Because I feel I'm responsible for a mistake.

MEV:

LD: Yes, María Esther, I know. I shouldn't be telling you that I'm the one who's most affected, the most injured party is yourself. But in the D'Onofrio case I sincerely regret what happened.

MEV:

LD: It's not because you have a whole career behind you, that doesn't matter.

MEV:

LD: No, neither does it matter that you're almost sixty years old, what matters is the work presented to the jury.

MEV:

LD: You make me feel very bad, you shouldn't say that to me.

MEV:

LD: But I've tried everything to convince the jury, and they don't listen to me, the decision is already made and they can't change it. The only way of fixing things . . . would be something else. I'm going to continue trying.

MEV:

LD: Yes, there is a way.

MEV:

LD: The way is that she'll give up her chance to take her works to São Paulo.

MEV:

LD: No, it's not too late.

MEV:

Leopoldo Druscovich's apartment, May 5, 1969

LD: (on the telephone) It's me. Did I wake you up?
MEV:

LD: You sound as if you'd been sleeping.
MEV:

LD: Forgive me, but I had to talk a bit, I don't feel well.
MEV:

LD: Is it that late? (he looks at his watch) You're right, what a beast I am.
MEV:

134

LD: What did you see?

MEV:

LD: Was it good?

MEV:

LD: I wanted to see it, I read in an interview of Manzù that his favorite was Streisand, she's the only new discovery lately. I want to see *Funny Girl*.

MEV:

LD: No, it's horrible, don't see it. They didn't understand Poe, the Fellini episode is the worst, because it's the most pretentious.

MEV:

LD: What a genius? Not now, everything he does is old, pop Freudian symbolism, don't make me laugh . . .

MEV:

LD: I didn't go anywhere, I had a lot to do but just the same I didn't do a thing.

MEV:

LD: I stayed home for that, to work. I have a long article to do and it looks like I'm not going to be able to hand it in. Home all day Sunday and I still didn't get anything done.

MEV:

LD: Yes, on Friday we received a copy at the magazine and I read your interview.

MEV:

LD: I was surprised at those statements you made.

MEV.

LD: They seemed completely reactionary to me. How is it that at this stage of the game you have doubts about divorce and abortions? I don't understand . . .

MEV:

LD: What do you mean by that?

MEV:

LD: You've never regretted anything in your whole life?

MEV:

LD: That is, if the same situation came up again, you're sure that you'd do the same thing . . .

MEV:

LD: What you say frightens me.

MEV:

LD: Haven't you ever hurt anybody, really bad?

MEV:

LD: I don't know . . . Haven't you ever hit anybody, or injured anyone?

MEV:

LD: Haven't you ever wanted anyone to die? Because I have.

MEV:

LD: Haven't you ever felt . . . like killing someone?

MEV:

LD: Yes, you, didn't you ever?

MEV:

LD: Why don't you believe in repentance?

MEV:

LD: I lied to you. The truth is I voted for her because at that time we were having a relationship. It's not true that I gave her the vote before.

MEV:

LD: And where am I going to go at this time of the night? If I want fresh air I can open the window.

MEV:

LD: Talk a little more, then you can go back to sleep.

MEV:

LD: Don't hang up.

MEV:

LD: I get the impression that you don't believe anything I say. Why don't you believe me?

MEV:

LD: I want to tell you something.

MEV:

LD: No . . . I'm afraid to.

MEV:

LD: No, don't hang up.

MEV:

LD: I wish she'd die.

MEV:

LD: No, what I wanted to tell you was something else.

MEV:

LD: Really, it's something I can't forget.

MEV:

LD: But I assure you that every time I remember . . . I regret it.

MEV:

LD: Yes . . . a woman. How did you know?

MEV:

LD: I hurt her a lot. I was only seventeen.

MEV:

LD: But you shouldn't tell anybody.

MEV:

LD: No, then I better not.

MEV:

LD: You're right, it's not correct.

MEV:

LD: I promise.

MEV:

LD: I'll never bring up the subject again. I promise, really.

MEV:

LD: Okay, see you soon.

A bar, May 7, 1969

MEV:

LD: I feel a little better. My fever's gone. It must be your company.

MEV:

LD: No, I don't feel like going home.

MEV:

LD: If you come with me, okay. And we can talk and listen to music, if you like. I have a tape from Central Africa, tribal music. Before I forget, that color looks good on you.

MEV:

LD: You're afraid I'm going to make a pass?

MEV:

LD: Well, you're not that old. Don't exaggerate.

MEV:

LD: Well, if it's as you say that now a man means no more to you than a plant or a chair, come over to my house.

MEV:

LD: Okay, let's take a walk if you like.

MEV:

LD: No, I'm dressed warm, it won't do me any harm.

MEV:

LD: Really, I'm inviting you out, let's see a movie.

MEV:

LD: I would, but would you see it again?

MEV:

LD: You don't feel like seeing anything else?

MEV:

LD: Whatever you like, nothing then. Maybe you're right.

MEV:

LD: Yes, I'm going home to bed.

MEV:

LD: I should go see some people I promised to visit, but I'm tired.

MEV:

LD: No, but I have to go. Come with me.

MEV:

LD: You don't know them, I promised them some money and they called me now that they need it. Someone died and the wife and children need help. But I'm going to go another day. Unless you come with me now.

MEV:

LD: You're right. I shouldn't tire myself out, there's still time tomorrow.

MEV:

LD: But if I get home and I can't sleep I'll phone you, so promise me you won't complain if I wake you up.

MEV:

LD: Okay, but I'll drive you home.

MEV:

LD: Aren't you going home?

MEV:

LD: Then why don't you want me to take you?

MEV:

LD: Okay, then you call me. Call me before you go to sleep.

MEV:

Leopoldo Druscovich's apartment, one hour later

LD: (on the telephone) No, it's too late today, she's not going to call.

MEV:

LD: Yes, she called yesterday, I didn't tell you. I don't know why, I didn't want to bring up the subject.

MEV:

LD: No, she's already realized it.

MEV:

LD: She doesn't have the nerve for that.

MEV:

LD: She's not going to go to São Paulo, she wouldn't dare.

MEV:

LD: No, that's what I think. She didn't say anything.

MEV:

LD: Yesterday morning. She cried, it's the only thing she did, she didn't say a thing.

MEV:

LD: Pity for what? What she wants is to use me, what does she care about me?

MEV:

LD: What does she care about my problems?

MEV:

LD: She'd say yes to everything I say.

MEV:

LD: No, that's for lunatics, who want people to answer yes to everything they say.

MEV:

LD: My problems bothered her, that's all, she'd answer yes to everything.

MEV:

LD: That's why she doesn't dare contradict me, because she's afraid I'll get angry, and not give her what she wants, she's afraid that I won't let her use me.

MEV:

LD: She's always lost in herself. But I mean lost. She's always doing her thing but lost in it all. With her pills for sleeping and for waking up. Until one day she'll take them all together because that's what's going to happen. She's a potential suicide if I ever saw one.

MEV:

LD: You hate me, you won't forgive me for voting against you.

MEV:

LD: Don't say that to me.

MEV:

LD: You're always the one who hangs up.

MEV:

LD: Till tomorrow, then.

MEV:

Leopoldo Druscovich's apartment, May 8, 1969

LD: Since this morning. And now my fever's even higher.

MEV:

LD: Let's talk about something else. Explain to me your defense of the Argentine way of life, I think it's preposterous. Everything you said in that magazine.

MEV:

LD: Why did you pick on drug addicts?

MEV:

LD: María Esther . . . I can't let that woman get ahead. I can't tolerate the injustice.

MEV:

LD: If I feel better tomorrow . . . I'll call her up, and talk to her.

140

MEV:

LD: Yes, she's crazy, but nobody wants to admit it.

MEV:

LD: You have to go and tell her.

MEV:

LD: Talk directly to her. You have to tell her she's crazy and that she's in no condition to appear in public, that she can't assume the responsibility. Part of her work is her improvised conversation with the objects, and she's going to be tongue-tied in front of all those people. Tell her that, that she's going to be tongue-tied in front of all those people.

MEV:

LD: You have to go see her and frighten her.

MEV:

LD: If you don't see her I swear you're going to regret it.

MEV:

LD: You're going to regret it.

MEV:

LD: Don't leave . . . (he runs to the door and locks it from the inside)

MEV:

LD: You're going to regret it, because I'm going to do something crazy, and you could prevent it.

MEV:

LD: You're right, this is terrible . . . but only you can help me. You don't know how I envy you for being older and not having any more problems.

MEV:

LD: Because you don't have to rub against anybody to calm your nerves, I envy you that!

MEV:

LD: No . . . I won't let you go . . .

MEV:

LD: Promise.

MEV:

LD: Tomorrow for sure.

MEV:

LD: In the office, wherever you like.
MEV:
LD: But if I'm not well you have to come here.
MEV:
LD: You're positively going to help me?
MEV:
LD: Why should I believe you?
MEV:
LD: (he lets MEV go to the door and open it) Promise.
MEV:

Leopoldo Druscovich's office, May 14, 1969

MEV:
LD: I thought you were never going to call again.
MEV:
LD: You didn't keep your promise.
MEV:
LD: That's true, you're here.
MEV:
LD: You're going away?, for how long?
MEV:
LD: Please don't go.
MEV:
LD: Even if it isn't far, don't go.
MEV:
LD: I don't feel well, don't you believe me?
MEV:
LD: I have the impression that you don't believe anything
   I say, how bad I feel.
MEV:
LD: I'm not licking my wounds. Don't be unfair.
MEV:
LD: No, don't go, something happened . . . I saw her.
MEV:
LD: She cried.
MEV:

142

LD: That's all, she said that it wasn't my fault if I had stopped loving her, she said corny things like that.

MEV:

LD: She says that she still loves me despite the way I am, she said stupid things like that, that she loved me . . . Those very words. And she went to White Beach, where her mother is.

MEV:

LD: No, she's not coming back.

MEV:

LD: Yes, and she told me to burn her things, because she doesn't want to see them anymore, her collection of garbage.

MEV:

LD: Why should I be glad?, don't you see what's behind it?

MEV:

LD: It's all a trick. You don't realize it because you don't know her.

MEV:

LD: She's the one who's got to get rid of all that garbage.

MEV:

LD: Why don't you believe me? That's the way it is, I swear.

MEV:

LD: She's going to come to a bad end.

MEV:

LD: You're right, I can't even say her name.

MEV:

LD: Gladys! Gladys! Gladys! That ridiculous name.

MEV:

LD: I know she's going to come to a bad end, she's going to kill herself, I wish she'd killed herself already.

MEV:

LD: No, one day she's going to kill herself, I'm sure of it, but after all this is over, after São Paulo is over. She's going to ruin my life while she can.

143

MEV:

LD: What's wrong with me?

MEV:

LD: Why don't you like the look in my eyes?, what's wrong with it?

MEV:

LD: It must be the fever. I'm perspiring.

MEV:

LD: If you come home with me, okay.

MEV:

Leopoldo Druscovich's apartment, moments later

MEV:

LD: I don't want tea, throw it out.

MEV:

LD: No, throw it out.

MEV:

LD: It's not going to do me any good, throw it out I said.

MEV:

LD: (when he sees that MEV throws the tea on the jute rug) What are you doing?

MEV:

LD: I have something to tell you: there's a certain matter that frightens me . . .

MEV:

LD: That something will be found out . . .

MEV:

LD: . . . A certain thing I did, but without wanting to.

MEV:

LD: You're right, if I did it it was because I wanted to. Oh I don't know, no, that's not true, I didn't want to do it!

MEV:

LD: I'm sorry I did it.

MEV:

LD: Yes, you guessed right, another wreck like her. A long time ago.

MEV:

144

LD: No, I was never in jail.
MEV:
LD: No, nobody ever found out.
MEV:
LD: But just the same I'm worried . . .
MEV:
LD: No. It's just that something tells me that someday
. . . some complication is going to come up.
MEV:
LD: I'm going to tell you . . .
MEV:
LD: I don't know.
MEV:
LD: Please come closer. Sit here close to me . . .
MEV:
LD: Thanks, that's fine . . . Let me rest against you, let
me put my head on your lap . . . I'm going to tell you
something, but promise me that you're never going to
say a word to anybody.
MEV:

X

The old wardrobe woman: (in the dressing room of the chorus girls who are making their debut that night at the Ziegfeld "Follies") I'm supposed to be infallible, and I think there's no doubt that you'll reach fame.

Lana Turner: Thank you! (she turns around to look at herself in the mirror to touch up her extravagant attire)

Chorus girl: Now you must drink of the full glass, as tradition says.

The old wardrobe woman: Yes, drink the champagne from this glass, you're the chosen one.

Lana Turner: (as she turns around she unintentionally knocks the glass out of the old woman's hand, the other chorus girls cry out in dismay) I'm sorry, I hope this isn't a bad omen.

The old wardrobe woman: (trying to hide her profound fear) No dear, it's nothing . . .

Lana Turner: I was absent-minded, thinking . . . about love, thinking why is it the men we want are not the way we want . . .

(from *Ziegfeld Girl*, Metro-Goldwyn-Mayer)

The office of the Police Department described before. The officer has just placed the newly arrived evening paper on his desk, opened at the police chronicle section. His assistant, standing, also looks at the newspaper, over his superior's shoulder. The telephone rings, the assistant answers on his phone, located on the smaller desk. He immediately informs his superior that it's the same woman who had inquired about a psychiatric consultant days ago. The officer asks his assistant to record the conversation and gets ready to answer the call on his own phone. The assistant does not succeed in starting the tape recorder and without losing any more time he opens a notebook and grabs a pen to take down the conversation in shorthand. The officer gives the ready signal and starts talking. During the conversation his eyes repeatedly fall on the headlines in the newspaper—"Man Sets House On Fire With Girlfriend Inside," "Attempted Robbery Foiled, One Felon Slain," "Daring Robbery In Rosario: 4 Million Pesos Stolen," "Suspects Detained in Tucumán," "Four Sadistic Youths," "Ranchowner's Murder," "Woman Takes Own Life After Poisoning Her Two Children," "Free Lunch," "Operation Tucumán," "Urban Guerrillas Assault Bank in Villa Bosch," "Report on Urban Guerrillas"—and part of the text that follows each headline but without concentrating on the reading, paying attention only to the speaker. The shorthand version is as follows:

—Hello
—You not remember me
—Remember
—Very worried
—Speak freely
—Remember talk you my acquaintance, violent, consider dangerous
—Yes
—Now precise information

—Come here immediate no lose time, we all help possible

—No need me go, alarming information, can telephone, you decide later what do, what want

—No, you here, everything simpler

—No, waste time, person life balance, dangerous man, I no more responsibility, life danger

—Say man name finally

—I tell happened, not invented, you find name, don't inform cold-blooded, friend be enemy after

—Talk

—Man already other crime, years ago

—Continue

—He married '63 after premarital relations wife two years, always difficulty get along people, never able live anybody, wife work office magazine, good premarital, afraid live people always remember fights when young, he lose control hurt people classmate, violence problem

—Don't stop

—This informing

—Never arrested account fights?

—No, but not sure

—Go on, he marries

—Good premarital, friendship this woman, no commitment, free, no fidelity pack, that give hope, encouraged good sign dare marry, work together magazine, but live same roof man nervous, impossible live someone twenty-four hours day irritated, go crazy

—How you all this?

—Because he tell, I believe sincerity

—Continue

—Few months, marriage relationship bad, begin other woman, chorus girl, physical relationship, this woman how say, kept, almost prostitute receive money other men, older, money and appointments my friend intrude when another man come go pay bills

—What's name?

—Not dare, consultation not informer, I call him X, easier understand, X begin feel tied down carnally this kept woman, not tolerate frustration not see her busy other lover, day bell house without warning not find

—Wife know other woman?

—Yes, X tell all, separate wife, she leave magazine go live Europe, live Europe alone better die, want to return, X stay Buenos Aires, obsession kept woman increase when alone, one day go house without warning no find, accomplice doorman no information, X bribe doorman truth, doorman tell kept woman give order not let X enter because afraid X possessive jealousy, important detail, X make love marks body kept woman and official lover notice, lucky you don't see this moment because blush

—I not shocked, go on

—That night X watch front kept woman house located neighborhood dark streets trees

—Excuse, how X tell you, when?

—Already days ago, start tell, threats against other woman still not named, yesterday go his office find him sick ask go home with him, fear but pity, put to bed make hot tea, tell story, according X nobody ever know

X kept woman front door, continue

—Yes, she arrive taxi X approach, kept woman say not see X because afraid because life well-organized and X complications, worries not fun, X hug her but kept woman break loose ring bell desperation doorman, X feel ashamed run away reach corner turn slow down, one block there notice someone follow, a woman, ex-wife

—Not living Europe?

—Yes but return incognito those days call magazine then house without giving name fear rejected, not able find last attempt go house kept woman see there X crouched beast desire, not dare go near, she witness scene kept woman, prefer not interfere until X run away, then she follow till reach

—She not afraid?

—No, evidently in love, X say she accustomed X body, evidently she not able forget return to have relations, walk

149

begin caress dark streets X nervous after scene kept woman, talk nothing fear touch subjects not offend mutual feeling, suddenly X say better not touch, say good-by there, she bring hand to cheeks beg caress, X repulsed so that she forget pride desire, she hug tight, few steps vacant lot in dark, X struggle physical excitement and repulsion, she separate X and enter lot, high bushes cover, he not resist following, she throw ground unbutton clothes, X standing look begin undress, begin love, he impassioned but silent, suddenly she pull body away, she ask he say love her, he not say, he grab again, she deny body again ask declaration, he take force try continue act she struggle he superior strength gain control, she scream he frightened let go, moment motionless, he afraid some policeman rounds hear enter lot, seconds pass she tidy clothes he also dress wait moment if someone come lot but total silence nobody hear anything, she take advantage get up try run outside trip something fall ground, he reach hold down again she dressed but he tear clothes take her again, she threaten scream he tie shred clothes mouth completely out control she pull off gag threaten scream, he reach hand brick she struggle he want smash brick against face beside self, she relax arms finish taking off clothes, he gag again this time tighter knots desire destruction or rather self-destruction, she not move, he take her again, she no resistance at all eyes wide open, finish act he take off gag, woman not breathe, had asphyxiated

—What do corpse?

—Careful nobody see her get car go back lot, carry body travel hours river throw body place strong current

—Nobody concerned missing woman?

—Nobody know in country, he tell everything relive nightmare again die again enjoy again suffer relieved sleep finish story cry convulsively, all time during confession head my knees like child, I get up make tea already made other cup when arrive he furiously reject, now calm relieved, place pillow under head, he lying couch I return kitchen he smile couch, cups tea ask second cup, smoke one take out car accompany me home talk nothing whole ride smile, door house kiss forehead, return his house feel sleepy

—Very dangerous man, must give name

—Name Leopoldo Trescovich

—Spell

—D David R Rose U unique S Susan C Charles O Oswald V Victory I Iceland C Charles H Homer (here end conversation speaker hang up)

The newspaper texts that the officer read without paying attention were as follows: 1) MAN SETS HOUSE ON FIRE WITH GIRLFRIEND INSIDE—Santa Fe, May 15 (from our correspondent)—An irate man attempted to slay his companion, after an argument, by setting fire to the house. Abelardo García, a 45-year-old Argentinian, after a dispute with his common-law wife Ernestina R. de Peralta, Argentine, 50, closed the doors and windows of the slum dwelling that both occupied at 3457 Yatay Street, and after spraying it with gasoline he ignited it and fled. Fortunately some neighbors . . . 2) ATTEMPTED ROBBERY FOILED, ONE FELON SLAIN—Sarandí—Two men entered a perfume shop located at 2378 Laprida Street and threatened the owner, Ignacio Prado, with their revolvers. While this operation was going on and the culprits broke into the back of the store seizing jewels and money, the 4th Precinct received an anonymous telephone call, following which a police car went to the scene of the crime, eight blocks away, and arrived as the two men were preparing to leave. Caught in the act by the police the two robbers retreated and began to fire upon the policemen. The latter fought off the aggressors and one of the criminals was mortally wounded when . . . 3) DARING ROBBERY IN ROSARIO; 4 MILLION PESOS STOLEN—100 employees held at gunpoint—Rosario, May 15 (from our correspondent) Around 10:40 this morning, four men and two women assaulted the Persano & Co. firm, situated at 1800 Jujuy Avenue taking 4 million pesos, after which they fled and have not been located since. At the afore-mentioned time the assailants arrived at the place in a taxi, a 1964 Chevrolet, license plate RA 3075, and quickly entered the building. Two of them wore federal officers' uniforms and badges, and they carried small machine guns, while one of the women wore a blonde wig . . . These persons seized the money and left the place immediately driving off in the same taxi they had arrived in. Before doing so they freely handed out flyers printed in red ink and signed by a so-called Commando of Popular Revolutionary Action, "Liliana Raquel Gelin," where it says, among others things, that "we must experience the oligarch Persano so that his wealth will return to the people whom he . . . 4) SUSPECTS DETAINED IN TUCUMÁN—Tucumán, May 15 (from our correspondent) —After a spectacular chase two suspects, who last Dec. 12 assaulted the local radio station NX5, Radio Güemes, and stripped the policeman on duty of his weapon and uniform, were detained. They are Emma Laura Schultze, a 25-year-old Argentine student, and Raúl Arturo Rauch, a 26-year-old university student, also Argentine. The woman was on the wanted list for being an active member of an urban guerrilla cell and the man had been in prison for having participated in a guerrilla operation in Orán, in the province of Salta. Many weapons were confiscated, including those of the assaulted police officer, and the search for other accomplices continues since . . . 5) FOUR SADISTIC YOUTHS—The police of Bella Vista have solved a serious crime committed against a 26-year-old woman on the morning of May 2nd, with the arraignment of the perpetrators, who turned out to be four youths, ages 17, 16, 15, and 17. On that date the victim, whose name we shall omit for obvious reasons, reported to the police that while visiting the house of some friends, a couple, at 4 A.M. four boys, friends of the couple, appeared at the farmhouse in a car, and invited the three of them to visit another friend in the vicinity of Moreno. They accepted the invitation and the group undertook the journey in two cars. In one the couple and another friend, and in the other—a Fiat—the complainant and the four youths. When the visit was over they returned to Bella Vista but on route 5, leaving the town of Moreno, the aforementioned couple and friend lost sight of the other vehicle. The driver drove the vehicle toward a dirt road, then stopped and ordered them all to get out. Already on the ground, the boys attacked the woman and after beating her, they stripped off her clothes and submitted her to outrages immediately upon threats to kill her. The police detained the depraved youths and confiscated the vehicle used for . . . 6) RANCHOWNER'S MURDER—A Plane and a Woman, Keys to the Mystery—Mar del Plata, May 15 (from our correspondent)—In an atmosphere of justifiable secrecy, the investigation of the real motives behind the murder of ranchowner Antonio Romano, being carried out by the police and the Department of State Security, continues. Mr. Romano, 53 years old, was slain on his 16,000-acre estate, located in Mar Chiquita, by the young law student Norberto Crocco, a 28-year-old Argentine residing in Buenos Aires. Specialists in the Department of State Security are participating in the investigation because of increasing evidence that the deed was part of a plan devised by an extremist political organization. In effect, despite the secrecy of officials in charge of solving the mysterious crime, there have been reports to the effect that the terrorists' objective was to perpetrate an attempt upon the Air Force missile base installed on the Lake of Mar Chiquita; possibly Crocco's objective was to blow up the munitions depot on the base, which the terrorists probably thought would cause a sensational "impact" on public opinion. And Crocco must have entered Romano's estate because this entrepreneur and rancher was the only person—besides the military—who had access to the base. Romano had in his possession a key which permitted his entry and this privilege was the consequence of the confidence he enjoyed since the date he had offered his collaboration to the Army Air Force when the construction of the base was

. . . 7) WOMAN TAKES OWN LIFE AFTER POISON-
ING HER TWO CHILDREN—Berazategui—In a slum
dwelling of the Del Carmen fifth housing development,
Edelmira Barraza de Pintos made her sons Antonio Eufra-
sio and Froilán Pedro Pintos swallow nicotine sulfate.
After the boys' death had been induced the woman took
the same drug which also caused her death. At the scene
of the tragedy the police found a letter in which the
woman explains the motives that . . . 8) FREE LUNCH—
A Guerrilla Commando Distributes Free Meat and Another Makes a "Donation" of Milk—Córdoba (from our
agency)—Yesterday, milk; today, meat, and tomorrow,
what? the inhabitants of a shanty town district received a
free handout of meat, in the early hours of yesterday morning. It was barely dawn when loud horns disturbed the inhabitants of the Güemes district, a shanty town. At the
shout of *free meat for all!* from a truck the commando
summoned the people who rapidly flocked to the vehicle,
where the extremists began to hand out the produce . . .
Sánchez was driving the meat truck which belongs to
the "Albini" meat plant, loaded with beef to be dis-
tributed among its customers when at kilometer 3, on the
road to San Roque, four men got out of a Fiat 1500, joined
by another man, on bicycle, and intercepted the . . . 9)
OPERATION TUCUMÁN—In another operation in Tucumán, three men and a woman assaulted the driver of a
milk truck which carried 220 crates of milk and then dis-
tributed the produce in a shanty town by the railroad
tracks. There . . . 10) URBAN GUERRILLAS ASSAULT
BANK IN VILLA BOSCH—In a commando-type operation, which was executed in five minutes, eight men and a
woman, identified as members of the guerrilla organization known as Montoneros, yesterday assaulted the Villa
Bosch branch of the Hurlingham Bank S.A. After wound-
ing a police officer who was on watch, they held at bay
twenty customers and five employees and seized . . . 11)
REPORT ON URBAN GUERRILLAS—Córdoba—In this
city the report sent to headquarters by personnel of the

10th Precinct on the activities of the secret organization RAF (Revolutionary Armed Forces) has been made public. RAF has conducted several operations in this capital, among them a bloody assault upon the Air Force branch of the Bank of the Province of Córdoba. The extensive report indicates that as a consequence of the failure of an RAF operation against the Quilmes branch of the Bank of the Province of Buenos Aires, the national directors of the subversive organization arranged to transfer one of its members (identified immediately after the frustrated attempt) to this city. He assumed the name of Jorge Pedro Camalot and moved to 833 Castelar Street, in company with the so-called Laura Susana Kait (whose real name is Raquel Gelin). Both were assigned the task of recruiting members in order to create local cells of the organization. The initiates received as *noms de guerre* the pseudonyms . . . .

XI

The British planter: (to his wife, who has just confessed to
    him that she didn't kill a man in self-defense, but
    out of spite because he was abandoning her) We
    must stay together, it's all in the past now.

Bette Davis: (looking aimlessly at the flawless furniture of
    that Southeast Asia cottage, far out in the jungle) But
    can't you see. . . ? With all my heart I still love the
    man I killed . . .

                (from *The Letter*, Warner Bros.)

                Night of May 19 to 20, 1969

Next, Leo's principal imaginary actions during his insomnia are listed:

1) In the living room of his apartment, on the rug, there
is a stain. It is a puddle of whitish, sticky liquid, but those
details are hard to distinguish because of the darkness.
The main door which leads to the hallway has been left
open and one can see a greyhound, with sores from sca-
bies on its legs, walking away and coming back again. The
greyhound enters, exhales hot steam from its snout, snaps
its tongue and discovers beside the stain a naked man
lying on the floor. The man doesn't move. If the man
moves the greyhound might leap and bite him. The grey-

156

hound puts its tongue in the puddle, from its snout drips the slimy liquid. The naked man brings his hand near his groin to cover it, the greyhound growls, the man stops his hand, with sharp, quick bites the greyhound could tear shreds of skin off him, producing intense hemorrhages. The man looks at a dark scabby spot on the greyhound's ribs. The latter sticks out its tongue, which from close up displays yellow buds in the form of polyps, and brings it close to the naked man's groin. The door of the apartment is still open, from the hallway one could watch what is happening. The man opens his eyes wide when he sees that, among scabs stuck to the grey hide, the greyhound has black and wrinkled udders. The greyhound sticks its tongue out even more, the saliva dripping out is as thick as the liquid in the puddle, the animal licks the man's groin, then his stomach, chest, and finally his mouth. The man remains motionless, he notices that under the neck is where the largest sore festers, overflowing with pus. One can hear footsteps on the stairs, the animal looks toward the door; on the floor, within reach of the man's hand, lies a slipper, the man sees it, stretches out his hand, grabs it and deals a hard blow upon the animal's udders. The animal lets out a muffled cry. Drops of blood flow which soon clot and become black like the udders. The animal crouches in a corner of the room, trembling. The man goes to the shower, turns on the faucet, picks up a piece of soap, produces abundant, white foam, carefully eliminates all dirt. The animal does not move from the corner, does not bleed, a colorless thread of drivel winds its way between its legs and dirties the floor. Moments later a neatly groomed couple walks along a wide and treelined sidewalk. It's a sunny afternoon. The couple is about to reach the corner. They have to cross the street. The traffic is continuous, it is necessary to wait by the edge of the sidewalk until the lights change. Vehicles of the city transit system quickly go by a few inches away and if he were to give her a dry and decisive push, three seconds before the passing of a rapidly oncoming bus, the victim would be run over.

But in such a case the bus driver would witness the maneuver.

2) A hotel room, apparently spotless. A sign on the street lights up and goes off again. A bed, fish skeletons, remains of a shipwreck, objects scattered in the darkness. Other debris: a torn rubber ball, smooth stones, the flaccid body of a woman lying on the floor. The sign lights up again, there are no traces of violence on the woman's body. The sign goes off again. On the contrary, in the stark light of the morning the police inspector runs his hand along the corpse, chamber maid and porter also notice that from between the legs a colorless thread of drivel drips on the floor. The inspector's hand touches the cold body and when it reaches the trachea he notices that it is broken. He explains that certain karate chops take lives without causing bleeding, in either victim or criminal. One by one the employees are submitted to questioning, all agree that they saw nobody go up to the room. The criminal has left no trace, there is the possibility that it was a crime of theft. The case is filed.

Until one hot afternoon an accusation catches the police authorities by surprise. Before sunset the informer is confronted with the accused. At the end of a dark corridor the accused sees a familiar figure appear, walking erect. The accused trembles with rage when he sees him approaching, he insults him, calls him traitor. The informer repeats his charges before the accused, violating professional secrecy and without material proof, only on the basis of psychiatric deductions, he accuses the man who at that moment has his hands bound in fetters. The investigators listen attentively, the doctor arches an eyebrow, lastly throws a mesmerizing glance at the accused. The crime is solved. The sentence is life imprisonment, for premeditated murder.

In his somber dungeon, days and nights are the same for the convict. Slowly in the dark the membranes of his retina atrophy, until becoming hard and cold like glass. Many years pass. The convict's hair has turned white when his pardon for good conduct arrives. The doors of the penitentiary open, a dog guides the blind man until they come to a very meager house. It is open country, a completely solitary place. For the old man there too days are the same as night, until he begins to distinguish them because when the sun comes out his malaise worsens, his headaches become intolerable. The dog does not leave his master's side, he seems to know that he's painfully sick. Under the midday sun his suffering increases and, like the retinas, part of his cephalic matter is turning to glass. It's a cerebral lesion, a deformation of the cells, the consequence of twenty years in total darkness. The dog leaves his side for the first time and runs barking for miles until he wakes up the occupants of the nearest house. Doctors with skullcaps and face masks carefully wield surgical instruments, trying to remove the tumor from its roots. They know that the operation is risky, it must be carried out with speed and precision. The gloved hands act with accelerated rhythm. But halfway through the operation their zeal is useless, a male nurse slowly takes away the patient's lifeless body. The trees around the isolated hut in the middle of the field are losing their leaves, strong autumn winds sweep them from side to side, incessantly. Some accumulate at the end of the orchard, and at moments cover the little mound of dirt that surrounds a wooden cross. Nobody hears the dog who howls there.

3) The plane takes off en route to São Paulo. One of the lady passengers is afraid of heights and holds onto her companion's arm. With difficulty he manages to hide a gesture of repulsion. He's a dangerous criminal. She doesn't know it. The cruising altitude reached, he impassively pushes back his seat to rest. Minutes before landing they can see the skyscrapers of São Paulo. The airport is filled with people. Passing through the immigration booth he finds out that an Argentine can enter Brazil with any kind of identifying document and that document is not stamped and dated by anybody: he concludes that the same thing happens on returning to Buenos Aires from an adjacent country.

Night falls early in the tropics, the clock in the International Exhibition Pavilion strikes six. Fish skeletons, remains of shipwrecks, also visible are a torn rubber ball, smooth stones, scattered objects. After hours of work under his direction, the corner of the hall where the work will be verbalized for the public is ready. He looks at the artist and tells her that he is no longer needed there, his task of organization is accomplished. She turns pale upon seeing him leave without further explanation. He reaches the airport, presents his ticket and the employee withdraws the corresponding coupon, only there does the traveler's name appear, in exchange he receives the embarkation card. One piece of hand luggage is all he has, in a few minutes the plane will take off, the impassive traveler buys a newspaper, on the overhead speaker a woman's voice announces the departure for Buenos Aires and the corresponding gate in several languages. The traveler appears at the gate and hands in his card as he should, but now on the ramp, surreptitiously, he separates from the group of passengers and hides in a hangar. The stewardess is at the head of the group and doesn't notice anything. The traveler has officially left the country at eight o'clock, the only controls being the embarkation card and the coupon with his name.

The traveler goes from that hangar to a corridor, from there to the employees' restaurant, he leaves his hand luggage in an automatic locker in the large vestibule of the airport, takes a taxi and goes to the hotel where she is staying, he has kept the key to her room. But he has to pass in front of the night porter's desk, go up the elevator, the elevator man recognizes him and is surprised to see him back, wasn't the traveler supposed to leave on the eight o'clock plane? The traveler goes from the hangar to a corridor, from there to the employees' restaurant, he leaves his hand luggage in an automatic locker in the large vestibule of the airport, takes a taxi and goes to the International Exhibition Pavilion. There's a guard at the entrance. He goes around and jumps over the wall, everything's in the dark, one hears footsteps, sees the gleam from a flashlight, she and the guard are coming down the corridor. He hides behind a column, the guard draws open one of the heavy canvas curtains and lunar light comes in, she says that she is satisfied with the inspection, the guard walks away with his flashlight. She is standing still, staring at her scattered objects. He tiptoes near and his figure is outlined against a window. She can't see him because she has closed her eyes, she has in her hand some debris from a shipwreck covered with rust, she holds it against her chest, murmurs the criminal's name in a loving tone. He answers her that he is there, present, she sees him and throws herself in his arms. He begins to undress her, she offers no resistance, he lays her down naked on the tiles, covers her mouth for fear that she'll cry out in pain and someone will run to her aid. She doesn't offer the least resistance, he penetrates her and she does not try to get away, but inexplicably the erection subsides and he doesn't know what to do. She and the guard are coming down the corridor. The criminal hides behind a column, the guard draws open one of the heavy canvas curtains and lunar light comes in, she says that she's satisfied with the inspection, the guard walks away with his flashlight. She is standing still, staring at some of her scattered objects, she starts talking to them, she says that she has achieved her goal by simply making use of a man's gullibility. She laughs sarcastically, the echo is reproduced in the half-empty rooms. The laugh stops short, she has noticed that among her debris a small rusty iron anchor is missing, she shudders, it is too late.

The patient notices a shadow of suspicion in his doctor's eyes. The latter does not express sympathy after hearing the confession of the crime. The patient is sure that the doctor is thinking up a plan. The patient closes his eyes, the street noises irritate him, keep him from concentrating on the flow of his consciousness, he complains of that to his doctor. The latter answers that the patient is disturbed by other voices, in his conscience, which he cannot silence. The patient fears that the doctor will betray the professional oath and inform on him to the police. The doctor promises him total discretion, but demands not to be taken for a fool since the murder of the woman never took place and she must be hidden in some secret spot, since the charred corpse found in the pavilion was not hers. The patient assures him that the corpse was not charred. The doctor says that after the murder the criminal sprayed the corpse with alcohol, burned it up, and that's why they'll never know who was killed, after the rape in the dark. The charred body, of a woman or man, could not be identified. The criminal assures him that he didn't burn the corpse and again asks him not to violate the professional oath. The doctor arches an eyebrow, throws a mesmerizing glance at the patient and adds that no professional oath links him to another crime, committed a long time ago. The patient pretends not to realize anything, at which the doctor gets irritated. The patient is motionless on the couch, his doctor adds that after sessions of analysis he has managed to find the key to the patient's personality, and that has led him to discover a perfect crime, committed in a vacant lot, many years ago. The doctor goes toward the phone, turns his back on the patient, picks up the receiver. Beside the patient there is a colored quartz ashtray, lighter than a brick. The doctor dials the usual six digits, seconds later the line is connected and a bell rings at the other end. Raw quartz has a rough surface, the arm deals a blow with all its strength and crushes the nape of the doctor's neck, an officer on duty answers the other end of the line, the criminal picks up the receiver and excuses himself for having dialed the wrong number. The doctor's motionless body lies on the Persian rug, the criminal tears the doctor's clothes, strips him almost naked and prepares to void his intestines on the dead man. But at that precise moment one hears footsteps: she and the guard are coming down the corridor. The criminal hides behind a column, the guard draws open one of the heavy canvas curtains and lunar light comes in, she says that she's satisfied with the inspection, the guard walks away with his flashlight. She remains standing, staring at some of her inanimate objects, she laughs sarcastically, the echo reproduces it in the half-empty rooms, the laugh stops short, she has noticed that among her debris a small rusty iron anchor is missing, she shudders, it is too late, she doesn't have time to turn around, a contracted hand thrusts an anchor with all its strength into her skull. The body falls lifeless, the criminal tears the woman's clothes, female organs appear in sight, the criminal gets ready to abuse the flesh of the dead woman. His warm skin comes into contact with her cold skin. The criminal twists his mouth into a rictus of pleasure, his jaws quiver. But at that precise moment one hears footsteps, the guard is coming down the corridor. The criminal is forced to interrupt the act. He flees, jumps over the wall, runs through the streets.

The São Paulo airport is almost deserted, the last plane of the night is about to take off, bound for Foz de Iguazú, a small Brazilian town near the Argentine border. It is a flight inside the country, they don't need documents, name, or any data, the ticket can be bought on board as if it were a city bus trip, and it still isn't dawn when the plane lands in the jungle. In the distance one can hear the waterfalls like a continuous thunder, a few steps away a river marks the natural border with Argentina. For a few dollars the criminal crosses it in a rickety smugglers' boat, he stares at the lights on the opposite bank. They are small colored lamps that stay on all night, indicating the location of a tropical brothel. The criminal enters, orders a drink while he looks at the heavily painted faces of the prostitutes. Soon it will be dawn, one can hear distant maracas and bongo drums. An old bronze bed, fading red lights, from his ring a parrot watches the couple. The criminal wants to put an end to that long night, the woman gets undressed and lies down, does not put up resistance, her legs are open. The criminal caresses her, the woman's flesh is flaccid. The criminal covers her mouth with a hand for fear that she'll cry out in pain and someone will run to her aid. The prostitute's eyes open wide, in a few minutes it will be dawn but the sky is still black. She trembles with fear, but for no reason, because he's already let her go, her flaccid flesh has repulsed him. The woman goes out of the room with a few bills in her hand and leaves the door open, he has no strength to attempt anything else, but he can't sleep without having expelled from his body the substance which poisons him, he looks at the open door, has no energy to get up and to prevent the greyhound from entering. The criminal closes his eyes, the greyhound has scabby stains, the greyhound licks him between the legs with its yellowish tongue, the night ends, the sun comes out and the waterfalls shine, the heavy canvas curtains are drawn, the sun lights up the vast hall where there are several scattered objects, such as rusty iron objects, pieces of rotten wood, a torn rubber ball, a bloody anchor, the shattered skull of a woman, bloodstains on the floor, a puddle of whitish, sticky liquid. The night has ended, the day begins, the greyhound steps into the puddle, leaves dirt wherever he steps, goes out of the room.

XII

Prostitute in prison: (she has listened with fascination, in that dungeon in Calais, to the long tale of an old thief who claims to be Lady Hamilton, the fabulous mistress of Lord Nelson) And when Nelson died in Trafalgar, what happened? You were still young and beautiful. What happened then?

Vivien Leigh: (whom nobody believes when she tells the truth, reduced as she is to stealing gin in order to try and forget her loneliness and poverty) Then?

Prostitute in prison: Yes, what happened after?

Vivien Leigh: There is no then, there is no after.

(from *That Hamilton Woman*, United Artists)

The office of the Police Department described before, May 20, 1969

Officer: And that's all. You must forgive us for making you come all the way here.
Leopoldo Druscovich: No, it's no problem. Thank you for letting me know.
O: Imagine, despite the fact that the accusation was anonymous we thought that there was something behind it,

and started investigating immediately. You really must excuse us.

LD: No, on the contrary, I'm grateful to you.

O: The communiqué from Interpol arrived yesterday, and with that we believe the case can be considered closed.

LD: You also work with Interpol . . .

O: Yes, we handle communiqués by teletype . . . That's how it was in your case. Wait a moment. I have the translation in one of these drawers . . . Excuse me a second.

LD: No, it's me you must excuse. Take your time, please. But don't let me keep you from your work. Leave it . . . if you can't find it.

O: No, I'm sure I saw it a while ago.

LD: I'm sorry to be such a bother . . .

O: Here it is . . . I'll read it: São Paulo, 5.19.69. Answering cable 438 of 5.16.69 re: Folio 38.967 we communicate result investigation citizen Amalia Kart de Silveira resident Rio de Janeiro presently here for organization Argentine participation in Bienal this year month July stop documentation permitted corroboration same person Amalia Kart ex Druscovich married in Carmelo Uruguay and dissolved same country by decision Civil Court of Montevideo docket number 17.897 date 12.7.64 stop the above-named stated being on friendly terms with ex-husband and does not know reasons accusation made at Police Department Buenos Aires and showed with authenticated papers actual work collaboration with ex-husband in relation Bienal stop"

LD: It's all true.

O: It was very simple, we made contact here in Buenos Aires with your ex-wife's family, they gave us her present address and Interpol did the rest.

LD: Very good.

O: Can you give us some clue as to the identity of the false informer?

LD: No.

O: Think carefully. If you have the slightest suspicion you

166

have to tell us, so that we can help you clear the whole case up, that woman has committed a misdemeanor by giving false information. She might continue to persecute you, she might cause you trouble . . . You have every right to defend yourself. You should even file suit against her for slander. According to her you are dangerous and occupy a position that you're not worthy of, also that you're not in your right mind and turn everything you touch into . . . what was it she said? what was . . . No, I don't remember.

LD: It doesn't matter.

O: If you can't think of who it could have been, let it pass for the moment. But be on your guard and call us at the first clue.

LD: I'm very grateful to you, I promise . . . if I find out something I'll call you . . . Now can I go?

O: Whenever you like, sir.

LD: And does the person who made the accusation already know about Interpol?

O: Yes, unfortunately we don't have the proper technical equipment, and we can't trace a telephone call, I mean, find out where they're calling from. The only thing we could do was to tell her the truth and threaten her with an investigation if she persisted. That was this morning when she called for the third time.

LD: Can I go?

O: Whenever you like. You are innocent of the death of your ex-wife, who's fortunately in good health.

LD: Well, good-by, and thank you very much for worrying about me.

O: It's our duty.

LD: Good-by, and thanks again.

O: That's what we're here for, sir.

LD: Good-by.

O: By.

Leopoldo Druscovich left the Police Department and walked to his car parked a little over a block away. He had to stop off at the magazine to pick up some official papers and from there to a government office to speed up transactions for the Argentine exhibition at São Paulo. Despite the urgency of the case Leo decided that first he needed to get out into open spaces to breathe some pure air. He drove to the docks, but when he reached the entrance he saw that the police were detaining automobiles coming from the harbor and searching them for possible smuggled goods. He backed up, turned onto a long boulevard and after thirty minutes of driving held up by traffic he reached the border between the capital and the province. He chose a four-lane highway and drove for twenty-five miles. He stopped at a roadside bar and had a soda. He asked to use the private telephone, there was no other, to inform his office that he was indisposed, and would not appear until the next day. But the call was long distance and there was no line open. He returned to the automobile, was about to start it when the waiter caught up with him to charge for the soda which, unawares, he had forgotten to pay for. He paid the bill and gave a tip equivalent to the expense incurred.

He drove at very slow speed back to the capital. When he reached the belt parkway he had to take a right turn to get back home, but he felt an uncontrollable revulsion and turned left. He entered a comfortable middle-class neighborhood. He saw a garage with a sign that guaranteed to wash the car in a few minutes and he asked how long they would take to wash it. He used that hour to take a walk. After several blocks he felt thirsty, entered an ice cream parlor and asked for a cone. The attendant asked him what flavor he preferred. The customer found great difficulty in concentrating; the list offered twenty different flavors. He was about to say that he had no preference but he didn't because he assumed that such an answer would seem strange to the attendant. He again looked at the list trying to concentrate, the first name said "lemon." He ordered it, and immediately thought that he had never liked it, he then stammered some words but didn't finish his sentence.

The attendant looked at him again but didn't stop preparing the cone, the customer kept staring at him, the attendant asked him to pay at the cashier and return with the sales slip. But in front of the cashier the customer couldn't find his wallet, in fact, he had left it inside the automobile, after paying the waiter at the rural bar he had placed it temporarily in the glove compartment. He took off his jacket and said that he'd leave it as security while he went to get the money. The cashier answered that it wasn't necessary but the customer left the jacket beside the cash register. He was already on the sidewalk when the attendant at the counter called out to him to take his purchase. The customer turned back and received the ice cream, walked off in great strides. He was very thirsty, he sucked twice very hard, the cold whipped the nerve endings of his teeth, he prepared to suck more carefully but from his tilted and trembling hand the dip of ice cream had fallen to the ground. His fingers held only the cone and upon falling the cream had stained his pants. A chill went through him when he saw the white traces somewhat below his fly and on his calf, the passersby might imagine something obscene. He looked for a handkerchief to clean himself, but the handkerchief had remained inside the jacket. He tried to clean himself with his hand. He walked to the service station at a brisk pace. In the bathroom he cleaned the few traces that were left with water, but since the pants from the crotch down were wet it looked as if he had urinated on himself. To prevent grotesque thoughts in the people who might see him he wet his pants from the crotch to his belt as well. The car washing had still not been completed, he decided not to wait and to return on foot to the ice cream parlor. A few steps before arriving he thought that his whole attitude had been suspicious, in the interim the cashier could have called the police and any further interrogation could be damaging. But the police car was not parked at the door, although it might arrive at any moment. He thought that if he hurried he could get the jacket and run out, the owners of the ice cream parlor

169

could not detain him without a written order or without a weapon. He walked faster and entered decisively. He paid, got his jacket, said thanks and once on the street walked quickly to the corner, turned, and finally out of the ice cream men's field of vision he sprinted away. He turned at each corner, running three blocks without halting. Exhaustion forced him to stop, he leaned against a tree. By then his reasoning, in summary, was as follows: María Esther Vila knew that he hadn't killed a woman; María Esther Vila, having discovered that he hadn't killed a woman in a lot, could conclude that he had committed some other, different crime; one more phone call to the police inspectors would put them on the track; the investigation would include questioning his acquaintances, among them his doctor, who would remember that the accused, when a teenager, had done something violent with a brick.

He stayed by the tree for several seconds, recovered his breath, and went to get his car. He drove with extreme prudence for fear of being stopped by a traffic officer, which would mean showing his identity cards. Upon reaching the corner of his house he decreased the speed a bit, from there he would be able to sight police vehicles parked in front of his door but he didn't see any. Nevertheless he continued to go around the whole block before getting out. He went slowly around the other corner repeating the operation from the opposite visual angle. There was no evidence of police vigilance. He parked the car two blocks away and, pretending to be calm, he walked to the door of the apartment house where he lived. By then his reasoning, in summary, was as follows: if he killed a woman he could show María Esther Vila that that had always been his intention, and once convinced of his true intentions the above-named would stop investigating the crime of the vacant lot.

There was nobody at the street door, after nine at night the doorman locked up and retired until the next day. The elevator was on the last floor, he preferred not to stay in the hallway waiting for it and went up the stairs to his apartment. Before entering he looked to see if there was a light under the door. It was dark. He moved close without making the slightest noise and stuck his ear against the door. He couldn't hear any voices or footsteps of supposed investigators searching through his belongings. He entered, did not lock the door nor bolt the latch from the inside in case he had to suddenly escape—someone might be waiting for him behind the curtains, inside a closet, under the bed—, since unbolting the latch and turning the key would make him lose time. He searched the house, nobody was there. He prepared a glass of whiskey with ice, he was about to drink it when he thought that he might have to resort to barbiturates in order to sleep that night, and mixed with alcohol they could cause death. He spilled the whiskey into the bathroom sink, let the water run to remove the smell of liquor. By then his reasoning, in summary, was as follows: he had to convince María Esther Vila that his intentions had been otherwise, and to do that, María Esther Vila would have to arrive at the place of the crime and discover him with his victim recently finished off; by means of a maneuver he could make it look as if María Esther Vila herself were guilty: if Gladys Hebe D'Onofrio were murdered and her most obvious rival was found at the scene of the crime, suspicion would undoubtedly result; but even if that plan seemed logical it would be difficult to plot it without the risk of going to jail for life.

Suddenly he noticed that he already had his sleeping medicine in his hand, he didn't remember having looked for the bottle, having opened it and counted the usual dosage of pills. He concentrated and then succeeded in remembering that after rinsing the glass of whiskey he had taken a drink from the same glass. Had he taken water to swallow the pills which he had unconsciously brought to his mouth? He decided to abstain from a possible second dose. He telephoned Gladys' hotel, they replied that she had already returned to the coast several days ago. He finally asked what he was really interested in, that is, if she had made any reservation for an expected return, and they answered no. They asked if he wanted to leave some message or simply his name, he answered that his name was Eduardo Ramírez and that he was looking for her to propose an art exhibit in a gallery in the city of Rosario. He invented that data for fear of seeming suspicious if he refused to leave word. He hung up, remembered with relief that in the Police Department they had told him about the impossibility of tracing telephone calls. By then his reasoning, in summary, was as follows: if María Esther Vila came to the place where the crime was about to be committed—it was he who was going to kill a woman—and she prevented it—apparently—with her unexpected presence, she would no longer doubt his intention to kill a woman; thus preventing the murder of a woman at his hands, María Esther Vila would be convinced that the crime in the vacant lot had been of the same sort.

XIII

The Austro-Hungarian general: (in his bachelor's den after the masked ball) Champagne?

Marlene Dietrich: (removes a pistol from the spangles of her costume, aims it at him) No.

The Austro-Hungarian general: (suddenly realizing that the girl is a spy and has discovered the secret message contained in an insignificant cigarette holder) I guess the block is already surrounded by the police.

Marlene Dietrich: I'm sorry, it's my job.

The Austro-Hungarian general: (sincere) What a charming evening we would have had, if I hadn't been a traitor and you a spy.

Marlene Dietrich: (nostalgic and disenchanted) In that case we would have never met.

(from *Dishonored*, Paramount Pictures)

The night of May 20, 1969, Leo conceived his plan of action and immediately arranged to carry it out. Driving at a high speed he reached White Beach before dawn and parked the car twenty yards from the house where Gladys lived. He jumped over the garden hedge without any difficulty and went to the backyard where the barred window of one of the bedrooms was located. The shutters were fastened to one of the window panels but the panels were only partially closed. Leo stuck his arm between the bars and pushed one of the window panels. Immediately on hearing a slight noise, Gladys sat up in bed. Leo whispered to her not to be frightened, it was only a friend. Gladys had often imagined that Leo would one day come to her window. He asked her to come outside, he didn't want to wake up her mother. Gladys had no interest in waking her up either, but she preferred Leo to come in. Besides, her mother's proximity would prevent Leo from having a fit of violence, she still remembered his threat to beat her during one of their last meetings in Buenos Aires.

Gladys went on tiptoe to the front door and let Leo in, her finger on her lips as a signal of silence. Leo followed her to the bedroom but there, in a very low whisper, he said that he preferred to talk to her in his car, parked close by. Gladys had never made love in a car, felt curiosity and thus agreed to go out. She was afraid of making noise if she got dressed and preferred to go out in her nightgown, she looked for her slippers but couldn't find them in the dark, she preferred going out barefoot because turning on the light would be dangerous. She took a coat from the hanger in the hallway. Once in the car Leo pulled out a Scandinavian flask filled with Gladys' favorite drink, Planter's Punch, a Caribbean cocktail made of rum and fruit juices. Leo was telling her how sorry he felt about everything that had happened, Gladys fell asleep. The cocktail, which Leo carefully prepared with dissolved sleeping pills, had taken effect. Next came a risky maneuver, transporting Gladys to the back seat. Leo looked in all directions and didn't see anybody nearby. In any case it was risky to take her out of the car in his arms and place her in the back, he decided to do it after getting on the highway, deserted at that time of the night.

At nine in the morning he was already in the city in front of his house. The few passersby who were out did not see a woman sleeping on the back seat in an uncomfortable position. The next step was the most dangerous, from the underground parking lot of the building he had to take the girl up to his floor. As soon as there was a moment of silence in the elevator shaft, Leo pressed the button. The apartment was almost dark, Leo deposited Gladys on the bed, stripped her naked, gagged her with a scarf and bound her hands behind her with a mourning tie that he didn't plan to use anymore. To carry out the rest of the plan he first had to call María Esther. But at that moment Leo had to face a complication in his plan: he was assaulted by an unexpected desire that was difficult to control since Gladys, naked and drugged, was unable to resist him. He got an urgent erection. He went to the bathroom and soaked a piece of cotton in chloroform, he applied it to Gladys' nostrils to prolong her sleep. He was taking off his shoes when the telephone rang. It was María Esther, her voice sounded fearful and guilty. Leo attributed his friend's new tone to the fact that she suspected something atrocious about the crime in the vacant lot and therefore he deemed it necessary to complete the plan without delay. In fact, he told her that Gladys was there, that the girl was lying unconscious and that he was no longer responsible for his actions. María Esther asked him why Gladys was unconscious. Leo answered evasively: only María Esther could prevent a tragedy, she must rush to his side.

During the twenty minutes it took María Esther to get there Leo finished getting undressed, wrapped a towel around his waist, soaked a piece of cotton in alcohol in order to awaken Gladys partially, placed a red vial of liquid vitamins on the kitchen counter, emptied another vial of vitamins, this time yellow, into the sink and placed the metal box of the hypodermic needle on the stove. María Esther would have to be extremely alarmed. He returned to the room, in the dark he could see the Moroccan knife that María Esther had praised so much on the occasion of another visit. Surely she would remember it and pick it up to defend herself. Leo hid it under the bed. The

175

set of Chinese needles on the other hand would not be useful to her as a weapon of defense, he left it on the desk. He forgot however to hide the Toledan scissors, half-hidden among newspaper clippings. When he heard María Esther arrive he grabbed the revolver, made Gladys smell the cotton with alcohol to wake her up and opened the door, without showing himself. María Esther came in, she didn't seem to have with her any weapon for defense.

Sensations experienced by Gladys in the presence of Leo and María Esther—Landscape: a luminous, nocturnal sky, in a tone similar to the aquamarine, that is, blue and transparent, the precious stone despite whose dense color one can see the insides of its setting and in the background the pale skin of the finger, the neckline, or the earlobe. Despite its transparency nothing can be seen behind that sky as if behind it there were nothing. Unusually bright stars are in the foreground, there is no moon. The earth shows no signs of life, a granite plateau and extinct volcanos. The granite is dark grey, with lighter veins and other darker ones, the volcanic craters are white but not from snow, rather a homogeneous substance which, like opaline, softly reflects luminous light rays. But nothing moves, there's no wind, the dust remains motionless like the rocks and stars. There are no petrified forests, decomposed wild animals, or human remains, in sight. Perhaps they lie buried beneath thick layers of lava. Looking back toward space one discerns that the stars are twinkling, thus an indication of energy. The total calm of the landscape is accented by string music, mainly violins. The tune is catchy, romantic, but with a background of dark foreboding.

Sensations experienced by Gladys upon noticing that Leo grips a revolver and María Esther remains silent—A danger: in a necessarily previous period of time, not corresponding to that of the landscape, a beautiful girl sketched with a few pencil lines on a white background, with blonde hair and a lock over one eye, discovers that her life is being threatened. She is the next victim. The blonde girl takes shelter from the rain beneath the awning of a store, in spite of feeling the presence of adverse forces nearby, she cannot tell where they are embodied. The previous victims were also unable to tell. Her retina does not acknowledge the radiance produced at isolated moments by a white homogeneous substance which softly reflects the astral light, young bodies might not perceive the possibility of an unfavorable occurrence, and might expose themselves. One waits for the moment in which the appointed victim finds herself in the open. Suddenly it stops raining, the sky is completely clear, the stars shine. The girl decides to continue her walk, on that street without traffic, open only to pedestrians. The wet asphalt shines, duplicating the fluorescent signs.

Sensations experienced by Gladys when Leo again applies the cotton to her nose to which María Esther does not react The beauty of those stars can be rated as dazzling, without that diminishing their possible evil power. Perhaps the conductor of the poisonous current is the air entering the lungs. The previous victims deeply breathed in the night air, their faces twisted into helpless grimaces, their eyes were shot with black and their lips split. The blood had frozen and burst the veins that could no longer contain it. The last victims managed to open their eyes slightly, they glimpsed the granite plateau, then a distant splendor of craters shed light on their last gesture, of intense pain.

Sensations experienced by Gladys when she hears María Esther ask Leo "What are you going to do?"—The blonde girl is walking down the street, the downtown area of the city is overflowing with people, she thinks that if something bad happens she will be able to ask any passerby for help. She no longer has any doubt that she is being observed, from where? someone must pass along the signal, only a person capable of recognizing her on the street. Therefore the girl is not afraid of any stranger, nobody in the city knows who she is. Consequently the girl is afraid of finding a familiar face. The lighting of that main street has an almost daylight effect, the city streetlamps, several yards high, curve at the top, the mercury lamp is protected by an aluminum screen which multiplies the luminous effect. On the contrary, the store signs are neon lights. There are horizontal ones, topping the display windows, but these are generally lit by sources of light hidden behind elements of decoration. The blonde girl notices a growing hum, looks at a shoe store sign and sees that between two letters a short circuit is about to occur, small sparks appear intermittently. She goes into the store and tells the attendant, he answers that this failure has been going on for days, but that it's not dangerous, the electrician will probably come by to fix it that very afternoon. The girl is back on the street again, she has found a certain resemblance between the attendant and someone she cannot seem to remember, or has she already seen the attendant on some other occasion perhaps? She turns around, he himself is looking at her from the door of the shoe store, under the lighted sign which is duplicated in the wet asphalt.

Sensations experienced by Gladys when she hears Leo answer María Esther "I'm going to kill her"—A physical disturbance: the chill that is being generated in her blood—now close to freezing point—equals the action of thousands of tiny metal filings—moving toward a fixed magnet—scattered inside her body, preferably in her temples, throat, and heart.

Sensations experienced by María Esther when she asks Leo "Why?" and he turns around without answering her, showing her his broad, naked back—A geometric figure: the height is a third of the width, it has no edges, the height line forms a ninety-degree angle with the plane or terrain upon which it is raised. The reverse side of the above-mentioned vertical plane is similar to those of the canvases used for traditional oil painting. The front side is smooth, off-white. The plane or terrain seems horizontal at first sight, but it is really slanting, to permit a better view for thousands of spectators, since there the traffic was cut off because of a bloody automobile accident a few hours earlier, and it's been decided to take advantage of the circumstances to present a mass spectacle on that temporary surface or screen, whose use will perhaps become permanent.

Sensations experienced by María Esther when Leo says to her "You're not going to tell anyone," and shaking Gladys to wake her up he adds "I want her to know that she's going to die"—Perhaps a live inaugural program will be on the screen, broadcast directly from the scene of action, a few miles away. The cameras which will record the event are already hidden behind a piece of furniture in a dark bedroom. Despite persistent rumors, the fatal traffic accident has nothing to do with the show. Precisely, the latter has been improvised because a large audience has gathered at the place, eager to see intimate details of the tragedy, and to whom an extra, or compensational distraction can be offered.

Sensations experienced by Leo, upon seeing himself in the mirror next to Gladys, motionless in the bed, and next to María Esther, who standing in the middle of the room, under the threat of his revolver according to the plan of action, exclaims "Please don't do anything crazy"—An identification document: the paper is of good quality, oaktag with slightly serrated edges, a sheet somewhat smaller than the size of a diploma. Leaving about a half-inch margin, a panel of small green laurel leaves frames the text, composed of black letters in Roman print. The largest are in the middle of the first line and say Birth Certificate. The following lines establish the fact that the bearer is the son of a gentleman and his legitimate wife. The data is added in blue ink. From the date and place of birth one concludes that the bearer was not forced to participate in any war, and that he has had the benefit of an educational system which made possible his free university preparation. Besides, the care with which the document has been preserved indicates that fortunately the child has been brought up in a tidy household.

Sensations experienced by Leo when he notices that Gladys' eye looks at the curved bulk formed by his sex organ under the towel—A freak of nature: the old manor does not have central heating and for the baby's bath special precautions are taken. An hour before, the kerosene heater is already lit and they've closed the windows and doors. Footsteps approach from the living room, the door opens and a nurse, or wet nurse, or very young aunt comes in. The mother slowly follows her, staring straight ahead with the baby in her arms; another nurse or wet nurse or very young aunt completes the group and closes the door behind her. The mother continues staring into space, one of the nurses takes the baby from her arms to remove his clothes and place him in the basin, an act which the mother cannot perform since she is blind. The other nurse puts her hand in the water to check the temperature, makes an affirmative gesture to her colleague. The latter observes the white foam and looking in another direction undresses the baby and puts him in up to his chubby, pink little shoulders. The mother asks them to bring her to the basin and allow her to scrub the baby. The two women give each other a look and advise her not to because the child moves and can slip.

Sensations experienced by Leo, when he notices that María Esther too is looking at the same place—The mother insists, assures them that she will be careful. One of the nurses brings her over to the basin and places the sponge in her hand. The mother begins to wash the little blond head with loving care, not even the soapy water manages to smooth down the many curls. She then washes the arms and graceful armpits, embellished by one or two little dimples, then the nipples and little belly button. One of the nurses tries to take the sponge away from her, the other says that it's enough, the baby is already clean. But the mother wants to finish the job and is determined to oppose anyone, because she hears the child laughing and reacting merrily to his mother's care. A grimace of disgust and fear disfigures the blind woman's face, the nurses can only accept what is beyond recall. One of them lifts the child from the basin and places him on the towels that are ready, trying not to look at the monstrosity before her. That baby is not normal, a man's sex organs hang from his curly pubic hair, and mixed with the white foam, thick drops of semen drip from the reddened penis.

Sensations experienced by Leo, upon María Esther's surprising movement when she takes hold of the virile member under the towel (led by a confused attempt at reconciliation) and says "What do you have here? a little birdie?"—A famous piece of sculpture: the ideal of grace and elegance pursued by the art of the IVth century B.C. is especially reflected in Hellenic sculpture. A beauty subtly impregnated with melancholy characterizes Praxiteles' divine images. Light slides along the surface of the bodies, Praxiteles preferred to use marble because of the luminous possibilities that it offered. Among the ruins of Olympia one of his masterworks was found almost intact, the naked figure of the god Hermes. Originally a symbol of fertility, he then came to inhabit Olympus as a divine messenger, later to be called Mercury in Roman mythology. Praxiteles' interpretation is characterized by such perfect beauty that it reaches the boundaries between dream and reality, the modeling is languid and voluptuous. In the expression of the face there is a dreamy hesitation, like a barely percep tible vacillation between impassivity and meditation. In the works of Praxiteles, especially this one, one can per-

181

ceive a spirit not tied to the severe norms of life which had characterized Greek civilization in all its splendor. Hermes' proportions are perfect and the work is almost intact, only the right arm and the virile member are missing, but from the realistic dimensions of the testicles and the proliferation of pubic hair, one concludes that Praxiteles must not have followed the norms of his predecessors—who contended that the minimized representation of the male genitalia was a sign of good taste—and therefore must have provided the god with a vigorous organ. But because of the mutilation suffered, this detail is confined to the sphere of conjectures.

Sensations experienced by Leo when he notices that his member, still in María Esther's hand, enters slowly into erection—A famous painting: Pope Sixtus IV built a chapel in the Vatican and its walls were later covered by Michelangelo's frescos. In one of the principal sections four hundred figures represent the Last Judgment. More than half of the space is occupied, above, by the celestial world, with Christ the Judge in the middle, beside the Virgin Mary; below are the judged souls that rise to heaven, and further below, to the left, those dragged down to hell, in the middle the angels who awaken the dead in their graves, and to the right Charon's boat. Near Christ, beside other saints, Saint Sebastian can be seen, identified by a bundle of arrows which he clenches in his left hand. In that way the painter wished to portray his station as a Roman soldier, head guard of the cruel emperor Diocletian. His physique is one of the strongest in the fresco, his chest is massive and almost square, his arms and legs very wide and not long. The gesture of his hands also indicates strength and determination. On the contrary his face is nobly sensitive, and curly hair falls on his shoulders. The tip of a cloth barely covers part of his groin, and takes the shape of the member it hides, definitely larger than that of the other male figures conceived by Michelangelo. Saint Sebastian stands out as one of the most beautiful, potent, and kind figures of the Last Judgment, painted soberly in several tones of ochre, beside other multicolored figures, and against the background of a clear sky.

Sensations experienced by Leo when María Esther lets go of his now stiff member, not covered but framed by the folds in the towel—The performance of a famous opera: in a cave in the forest the wicked dwarf finds a newborn infant and believes that he is the one the birds of the forest have announced to be the revenger of the mortals. Siegfried grows up in the forest and the dwarf teaches him the martial arts. He forges the invincible sword for the boy with the goal of eliminating the dragon of the forest, guardian of the treasure of the gods. The dwarf contemplates the young hero, endowed with superhuman strength, and decides that the day of combat has arrived. In the darkest part of the forest the dragon's den, a gloomy cavern, is hidden; the dwarf explains to Siegfried how bloodthirsty the monster is and how lethal the fear that he inspires. Siegfried asks what the word fear means. The dwarf answers that the dragon will make it known to him. The boy is not interested in the dwarf's chatter and orders him to leave him alone. Beneath the foliage of the trees he lies down to rest, there is total silence in the forest. Siegfried feels sad and doesn't know why, neither does he understand the meaning of the word loneliness. He never knew his parents and thinks of their faces which are unknown to him. The birds in the forest take pity and begin to sing to cheer him. The boy wants to accompany them in their song and with a reed he improvises a flute. But the sounds are too soft. So then he picks up his silver horn and plays a tune. The gay, boisterous song wakes the dragon. He comes out of his cavern to destroy the unwary one. Siegfried sees him appear, his hand is as firm as always, the hero does not know what it is to tremble with fear. He leaps near and thrusts the sword into the monster's throat. The latter, dying, relates to Siegfried that upon his sword a perfidious destiny will forever fall, since there is someone who lives only to procure his death and recover the sword. The dragon dies, his blood covers Siegfried's hands and seems to burn them. The hero raises his hand to his mouth, and then acquires a new power: he understands what the birds are saying in their song.

Sensations experienced by Leo when he notices that María Esther is smiling at him—A lark sings to him from his nest and says that in the treasure guarded by the dragon there is a magic ring. The hero puts it on his finger and calls the dwarf to show him the treasure, but the birds warn him that the dwarf is a traitor and will try to poison him. Siegfried refuses to believe it but when he sees the dwarf offering him a refreshing drink, the boy suspects what is behind the deceptive gesture, accompanied by words loaded with envy. The drink is a poison destined to kill him so that the gnome will become the master of everything. Siegfried cannot believe such infamy and turns around so as not to look at him, but unintentionally he sees the dwarf reflected in his sword, with a grimace of hate in his atrocious face. Siegfried, with a sudden blow of his weapon, kills him. The beasts of the forest roar with joy. The birds are silent, the hero is in the middle of the stage, the most powerful spotlights in the theater shine on him when, to the spectators' amazement, he takes off the lion skin covering him and is naked, Wagner's majestic music drowning the cries of admiration and shock in the audience. Siegfried will bathe in the dragon's blood and become invulnerable.

Sensations experienced by Leo when he caresses María Esther's cheek—The forest murmurs are very gentle. The hero again feels sad and asks the birds about his parents. The birds answer that they have died, but that there is another being who awaits him. It is a woman. She is asleep, surrounded by high flames way up on a mountain. Only a fearless man can rescue her. Siegfried does not know what it's about, he has never seen a woman. A bird leaves its nest, draws a circle with its flight and tells the hero that it will show him the way. But it also asks Siegfried to cover himself, because his vigorous, driving, extreme masculinity would frighten the daughter of the gods. The bird seeks the way in the thick of the forest and the hero follows it, in pursuit of happiness.

Sensations experienced by Leo as he sets aside the revolver on the bed next to Gladys' feet—But the night is shaken by storms and the circle of fire crackles menacingly. Siegfried protects himself with the helmet found in the dragon's treasure and goes through the flames. From the top of a rock he looks at the sleeping body covered with a warrior's cloak. He approaches it and takes off the cloak, it is a naked, different body. He finally knows what a woman is. He is seized by an emotion totally unknown to him. He trembles. A woman has taught him what fear is. A sleeping woman. The boy speaks to her, asks her name, but she is still submerged in sleep. Her white, delicate skin reminds him of certain flowers in the forest under the moonlight, which one must touch very gently, if one doesn't want to strip them of their petals. He touches her, caresses her lightly and discovers that her lips are rosy like a fruit. To taste their flavor he brings his own lips near. They don't seem to have a flavor, but they are pleasurable to the touch. Siegfried then inserts his tongue to taste them better. It is then that she wakes up out of her lethargy and looks around at the world that had been taken from her, by divine command. An invincible man has returned her to life.

Sensations experienced by Leo upon taking off his towel and looking at Gladys—Siegfried, overwhelmed by a blind impulse, tries to embrace her. But she slips out of his arms. She has been a goddess and no man has ever touched her. She does not know that the kiss has transformed her into a mere woman. He watches her run within the flaming circle and he is enraptured by her grace and beauty. Then he decides to take off his lion skin, so that the flames will shine on the two different bodies. The audience at the gala performance holds its breath. The maiden is frightened by the sight of a man's body, and tries to escape, she is light and can run swiftly like a gazelle. But Siegfried stops her and, while he kisses her, to hold her more firmly, he gently penetrates the white body. The girl tries to break way but it is too late. The audience feels outraged by such an obscenity and tries to leave the theater, but Siegfried prevents it, the usual exits are not where they should be, imperceptibly the opera house has turned into another enclosure, there is no exit in sight, and that place now looks more like the tent of a gigantic circus.

Sensations experienced by Leo as he reaches out and turns on a lamp that sheds light on the three persons gathered there—The two protagonists swing from the circus trapezes, as if they had wings, and look at the highest point of the tent with curiosity, they want to know if the canvas is cold there as they believe. They continue swinging and making daring turns from one bar to the next. Finally he stands on the bar of the highest trapeze, signals her to join him. She's afraid, but he insists. She gathers force and thrusts herself into the void, he must catch her with a perfectly timed swing of the trapeze. From there they will leap together to the highest point that the eye can see, they will somersault in the air and reach the rough but warm canvas of the greatest circus on earth. But the price of the feat may be very high, because the protective net has been removed and the bodies that fall into the center ring will pay with their life.

Sensations experienced by María Esther when Leo takes her by the hand and leads her to the bed—An application of platinum: in spite of its high cost, that metal is one of the most commonly used, occasionally together with iridium, in the making of satellites rocketed into space by commercial enterprises; those satellites revolve at the speed of the earth, therefore remaining as fixed stars at a given geographic point. The sun renews their necessary charge, since the photoelectric cells of the expensive metal capture the sun's rays, transforming them into electric energy. The satellite remains unchanged in its revolutions regulated to perfection, thrust from the earth by what experts in Physics call centrifugal force and which combined with the weight of the satellite itself results in a steady course.

Sensations experienced by María Esther when Leo moves Gladys toward the edge of the bed which borders on the wall—The new celestial body is a rebounding point, it will only be used to receive the waves sent from the earth—they must always travel in a straight line—and to guide them to a receiving center located on another continent, even enemy territory. Said enemy territory might or might not be interested in receiving them. The transmitting station will try all means possible to bring about contact. It will place the most prestigious images at the service of the transmitting antenna, and by means of variations in its magnetic field it will produce the modulations established by international agreements. Besides, that transmitting antenna has been unanimously recognized by experts as a masterpiece of electrotechnology. Its dimensions are gigantic and its special concavity, designated by a parabolic sector, is covered by a net of wires arranged like the cells of a beehive. But certain foreign powers still resist contact.

Sensations experienced by María Esther when Leo lays her down beside Gladys—A sudden worldwide upheaval: it is not known who has given the order to set off the transmission, all of a sudden the cells that were dark and empty are lit up, the wires burn brightly. First of all it is important for the satellite not to lose its initial speed and to continue following its orbit, if it stops it will fall to the earth like a mere stone, obeying the law of gravity. As to the enemy's reaction, that is impossible to predict.

187

Sensations experienced by María Esther when Leo raises her skirt, lowers her underpants, and caresses her pubis—But an image is already shining in space. Due to a technical difficulty the speeches cannot be heard, a buzz covers the voices. In spite of that, the expression on the face of the mature woman speaker is so intelligent, that the wise content of her words is taken for granted. On the other hand the cheap girls lying on the broken down cot, who reply in the next shot, reveal without having to be heard the banality of what they're saying. In these circumstances the superiority of what the mature woman expresses can be established without argument, since if one heard the speeches useless dialectic articulations could emerge.

Sensations experienced by Gladys as Leo gently but at the same time firmly spreads her legs, after kissing María Esther lightly on the mouth—Landscape: a field of rolling hills which form a horizon of wavy lines. Light brown earth, it is uncultivated, possibly dry, sandy. A hill somewhat taller than the others prevents one from seeing the region more clearly, only the hill is in sight, and behind it the clear, reddish sky of dusk. The few clouds that circle the sun do not predict a storm, they fulfill a merely decorative function, their edges are red and pink with golden reflections. There is total calm, the warm breeze seems to come from the west. A sound is suggested, a chirping of distant birds. One expects them to appear soon, but the hill continues to hide them.

Sensations experienced by Gladys when being compassionately but painfully penetrated by Leo—High on the hill a farmer with his plowshare appears. The birds follow, fluttering around him. The farmer's silhouette stands in front of the declining sun, since he's against the light one cannot make out his features, the ferocious or friendly expression on his face. The lines of his figure are strong and harmonious, his head is erect. Other additional details of a description would relate to the shirt with the sleeves rolled up almost to the armpits, and the overalls. That poor and sandy looking earth should be his next task, but it is possible he may avoid it knowing that it is barren. The farmer bends his head for the first time and watches where he steps.

Sensations experienced by Gladys as the pain ceases and she achieves a growing pleasure—The farmer is no longer against the light, one can clearly make out his features. It would be difficult to decide whether or not they're pleasant, because the expression that animates them in that moment is so affectionate that it would light up any face. The plowshare is sharp and rough, imperfect, forged by a hammer. The farmer moves forward with determination, he forcefully thrusts in the plowshare. The earth opens, the plow advances. Oh good man! with your sweat you till the future of our nation . . . You will throw the seed into the newly opened furrow and once it germinates the frail plant will bud, and then bear tassels to nourish all of humanity. You furrow the prairie with your plow, and you ask it from the bottom of your heart to fulfill a vow I, the earth, am in strife, but without moaning I bleed, and in barley, rye, wheat, and corn I give my life. Perhaps in your modest and virtuous attitude you will not comprehend your labor's magnitude, you sow the seed of love and friendship! Glory to thee, farmer! you forge with your toughness our beloved country's greatness!

XIV

Ginger Rogers: (prepares to go to bed early since she does
        the first shift at the armament factory, as a blue-
        collar worker; her baby cries, she takes him in her
        arms, holds him against her breast, on the night
        table is the picture of a soldier in the Second World
        War, with calm sadness she shows it to the baby)
        Little guy, this is your father . . . Chris, this is your
        son. You two aren't ever going to meet. Only
        through me will you ever know anything about each
        other. So now I'm making the introductions. This is
        your dad, young fella. You've got his eyes and his
        mop of hair . . . Remember him, son, remember
        your father as long as you live. He didn't leave you
        any money, he didn't have time, Chris boy. No mil-
        lion dollars or country clubs or long shiny cars for
        you, little guy. He only left you the best world a boy
        could ever grow up in. He bought it for you with his
        life. That's your heritage. It's a personal gift to you
        from your dad . . .

        (from *Tender Comrade*, RKO Radio Pictures)

Version that the doorman would give the landlord of the
building if questioned on the events of May 21, 1969, in
Leopoldo Druscovich's apartment

It was about nine-thirty in the morning and I was sweeping the sidewalk. Then a taxi stopped at the door and the people who got out asked me if I was the doorman. They were an older woman and a younger man, who I later found out was the son. Then they asked me if Druscovich's apartment was 8A and I said yes. I had no idea what was going to happen to me later. The woman saw that the front door was open, like every morning when I clean the entrance, and she went in without saying a word and the man stayed on the sidewalk. I noticed that she took the elevator. Some time went by, the man started a conversation with me but I don't remember what we were talking about, but I do remember that it had nothing to do with 8A. Some time went by and I was finishing my sweeping and I saw that he had already looked at his watch two or three times. It mustn't have been more than fifteen, or ten minutes, when the man said that I had to help him with some very serious business. He told me that Druscovich was very sick and that perhaps we should go upstairs to see if he needed help, because maybe his mother couldn't manage it alone.

. It seemed strange to me but we went up and in the eighth floor hallway I strained my ears to see if something could be heard from 8A, the door was closed. I didn't hear anything, and this young guy went to the door and knocked kind of softly and said "mama, is there anything wrong," something like that. We couldn't hear a thing, then this young guy said to me that his mother had gone up, but before that, she'd told him that if she didn't come down in ten minutes her son should go up and get her, because Druscovich was having a nervous breakdown and she was afraid of him.

The boy knocked and called to his mother again, and since again nobody answered, her son asked me to open the door, surely I had a duplicate key, maybe something had happened, Druscovich needed to be taken to a hospital immediately, Mr. Druscovich himself would be grateful to me for giving him the key. I could have told him that I had to go get them, the bunch of keys, but since I keep them with me in the morning right then and there I opened it myself.

There was Druscovich wearing nothing, with no clothes on, sitting on the bed looking toward the door, he covered himself with something right away, and there was a woman in the bed covered with a sheet, and this older woman who had gone up, kind of fixing her clothes, standing in the middle of the room. I saw that Druscovich had something hidden in his hand, and I thought that it was a revolver, but I wasn't sure. The boy's mother went out and I accompanied her and her son in the elevator. The mother said that she wasn't coming to that house anymore, and that she didn't want to have anything further to do with the matter, and they thanked me for opening the door for them. And I said to them what happens if there was a problem with Druscovich, what would I do, and the boy said that he would come back that very morning to talk to me, but that was yesterday and the guy never came back.

Then I said, I better go and apologize to Mr. Druscovich and I'll tell him everything that happened, that I thought he was sick. I rang the bell and said that I was alone, that the others had left. He opened it, he had nothing on, and I saw the rag that he had grabbed before to cover himself, and it was on a table, and next to it the revolver that I had already realized he had. The guy there naked and a woman with one eye sort of wounded, that she couldn't open, the woman that was still in the bed. But she was covered with the sheet.

I immediately said that I wanted to apologize for opening the door for that young guy, but that the young fellow had sworn to me that he was sick and we had to get in to see what was the matter. I was almost on my knees apologizing, because I saw in his face that the guy had a bone to pick, that I had put my foot in it, because you could see that he wasn't sick. He was nervous.

And then he starts laughing and says to the woman who was looking serious in the bed, keeping her mouth shut, she never said a word, he says that I didn't get a hard-on either, that he wasn't the only one. And he laughed, but you could see that he was in the mood for starting a fight. And he said that if she hadn't let go when we knocked on the door, they would have finished everything they had to finish, but that everything was fucked up now and it was her fault. And then he went over to the bed and pulled the sheet off the woman and she was naked. You could see she was afraid of him because she didn't even move. She looked like one of those cats when they're scatted by a dog and when they're about to jump but they can't. And he started in again, "see, he doesn't get a hard-on either," and then he told me to take off my clothes and take advantage of the opportunity, that she wanted it too. Well when I saw that they were both half crazy what I wanted was to get out of there, the woman had an ugly mug, but her body was kind of nice. And I didn't know what to do to get out of there, when he pushed me against the bed on top of the woman. And then I thought that I'd better leave as soon as possible and I told him I had things to do and I got up to go, and he pushed me against the bed again, but then I said that he should have a little more respect for me, that I put up with a lot with the tenants but he was overdoing it and God knows what else, and right then and there he grabs me in the balls and I almost double over with pain, and he said that my problem was that I couldn't get a hard-on and I got to the door the best I could, and left. Still kind of doubled over with pain.

About a half hour later he came down, I was doing the floors, washing the stairs between the top floor and the next, I was just beginning, and he appeared, you could see he'd been looking for me. And he gave me a big bill and said that he was drunk before but that he was over it now and was sorry. I grabbed the bill, because he had really put me through the grinder. And he said that he was going to be away for a day or two, and that that lady was staying in the house, if there was any problem she was there, and that's all, and he left.

193

After making his excuses to the doorman of the apartment building, Leo went to his office at the magazine. From there he called the committee in charge of the Argentine representation at São Paulo. He informed the person in charge that Gladys Hebe D'Onofrio was declining the offer to represent Argentina at that exhibition because she was not in good health, therefore they must immediately summon María Esther Vila to occupy her place. Since the winner had not yet been officially announced, as soon as María Esther Vila gave her consent they could inform the newspaper.

The person speaking to Leo said that personally he continued to be impressed by the originality of Gladys Hebe D'Onofrio's works, and that he would be interested in organizing an exhibition of the above-named as soon as she recovered, preferably in a certain new municipal gallery, which would be perfectly adapted to the kind of exhibit Miss D'Onofrio could offer. Before terminating the conversation he asked Leo to call him the next day because then it might be possible to suggest something more definite on the project, considering the person's friendship with the director of the aforementioned gallery. The person speaking also suggested that the news and publicity of Gladys Hebe D'Onofrio's first exhibition be published, naturally, in the magazine Leo wrote for, since he had discovered the unusual artist.

Due to lack of sleep the night before, Leo found it impossible to work; after forcing himself for a few hours he tore up everything he had written and left his office. He took a room in a downtown hotel, where he went supplied with sedatives. Given the fatigue he brought with him he tried to fall asleep without taking anything, but that didn't work. He thought of Gladys and of her difficulty in sleeping. He got up and opened the bottle that contained the barbiturates, he thought of Gladys' propensity toward suicide. He took two pills, a strong dose, and slept till the next morning.

He woke up with a headache. It irritated him to have to put on the same clothes as the day before. Without shaving he went to his magazine office. He could not concentrate on the work. The headache increased. There was a call from the person he spoke to the day before, to inform Leo that the committee had just announced the candidate to the press, the news would appear in the second edition of the evening newspapers. The person speaking also told Leo that he had talked to the director of the gallery, who was very interested in the project and wanted Leo to bring Miss D'Onofrio to his house that very night where from 10:30 on there would be a gathering of a group of qualified people.

The telephone conversation over, Leo called his apartment to speak to Gladys. He informed her that in the second edition of the evening newspaper the name of the artist invited to the São Paulo exhibition would appear. He assured her that it was a wise measure to avoid such a test in her precarious nervous condition. Gladys did not answer. Leo then explained to her that it would be more appropriate to begin with a less risky exhibit, before an audience who spoke her own language, and he ordered her to appear that night at the gallery director's house. He gave her the necessary instructions, assured her that he would not be present, and thus closed the conversation.

Convinced that he would not be able to work for the rest of the day, he delegated several tasks and left in his car in the direction of a highway that would take him out of the capital. He took route 9, toward Rosario. His intention was to drive until reaching open country, stop there and breathe fresh air. The high speed produced a pleasant effect in him, the continuous incidents of the road distracted him, and on one occasion, after passing on the right two vehicles in a row, he was even able to burst into laughter.

About one hundred miles from the capital, he passed a patrol station at a speed above the limit. The policeman on duty noticed him and tried to communicate with the policeman posted fifteen miles away, in the direction the car was going. It was impossible because the line was constantly busy and when he finally got through, his colleague had already seen Leo's car pass, also at a great speed, and had been unable to intercept him since he was busy with other tasks.

Leo experienced a gradual improvement and stopped at the roadside inn at the 125 mile point. For the first time in several days he had an appetite.

Leaving the inn he decided to return to the capital. By then his reasoning, in summary, was as follows: María Esther Vila, after having witnessed the episode of the morning before and—even more—flattered by the new nomination, would no longer persecute him with her suspicions; on the other hand, even though his plan had been fulfilled, unsolvable problems of another kind had cropped up again; despite that, the execution of the plan should be considered highly successful; as to Gladys Hebe D'Onofrio's disqualification, it was not an injustice, since she was not in condition to confront such a test, but since he had supported her initially, he should accompany her that night to the aforementioned party at the gallery director's house so as not to awaken suspicions; since it was advantageous for him to be seen with Gladys at the party, he himself should make sure that she appeared.

He increased his speed. When he passed the patrol station at the 105 mile point, the policeman caught sight of the car, recognized it, and immediately called the one who had seen it the first time and who could intercept it at the next station. It was already six P.M. when Leo passed the latter. He was going at an even greater speed, anxious to reach the capital in time to fulfill his new plan. Two policemen on motorcycles were waiting for him. As soon as he passed them they followed him. Leo noticed that the police had set out to detain him. He attributed this to the fact that the police had finally discovered the crime in the vacant lot, in complicity with his doctor and María Esther Vila. Leo increased his speed even more. When trying to pass another vehicle on the right, in a stretch near a curve, he lost control of the car and overturned.

Medicolegal Autopsy

Place: Baradero

Date: May 22, 1969

Name: Unknown

Description: Male, accident on route 9, driving car, overturned, car to be towed tomorrow, documents possibly inside car, left in ditch ten m. from this place.

Medical statement: corpse of a young man, in rigor mortis, skin white, hair brown, abundant on scalp, scanty fatty membrane.

By palpation and percussion the gross inspection of the corpse reveals: traumatic wounds on the face, deep lacerations; one of them on the upper lip, causing a hemorrhage in the gums, a large hematoma with flayings of the skin at the level of the right frontal region; another of the same size and form at the level of the temporal bone. Multiple contusions on the right leg, fracture of the femur in its middle portion, of the kneebone and of bones which form the instep of the foot.

By severing the tissues, with only a short surgical knife with a convex blade, through a deep opening of the skin and muscles, the following can be established: extricating the scalp by means of a hemi-section a hematoma can be observed at the level of the parietal bone.

Considering the posterior cranial wound, without extracting the cephalic mass, a fracture at the base of the skull continuing to the temporal bone can be observed. In the cephalic mass there are multiple ruptured blood vessels. Effecting a small vertical cut in the cephalic mass, one can identify exuding hemorrhages.

The femural fracture is explored through a deep incision on the anterior surface of the thigh. It is found adjacent to a large circular hemorrhage.

References omitted in the medicolegal autopsy

After death, the human body suffers changes of a general nature for all ages and races, except in the case of certain diseases which alter normal conditions. In Leopoldo Druscovich's body they found changes of a general nature.

Heart: within the first hours after death rigor is already initiated in the heart; it begins in the left ventricle, which empties out almost totally, and the right one of only half its content; in the first hour and a half following death, the blood of the heart remains liquid, then clotting sets in.

Blood: after death, the blood coagulates within the vessels; in cases of asphyxiation the blood remains liquid; then intestinal bacteria emigrate to the blood, where they multiply.

Brain: the processes of postmortem disintegration evolve very rapidly in the brain, they are recognized by the appearance of a greenish grey color in gas-filled cavities.

Oral cavity: the most important changes are those produced by desiccation if the mouth remains open; also dental impressions, determined by the cadaveric rigidity of the muscles of mastication, are produced on the tongue.

Teeth and maxillary bones: the teeth are very resistant, for that reason they frequently serve to identify corpses; the air and a high humidity favor their disintegration.

Esophagus and pharynx: above all the presence of impurities due to the passage of the stomach contents, which occurs during the agonal process and especially upon transporting corpses.

Bronchial tubes and larynx: ditto, despite the fact that they are not organs of the digestive but of the respiratory system.

Lungs and pleura: the stomach contents can also reach the pulmonary and pleural cavities after death, because of two different mechanisms: the acidic softening of the lung extends to the pleura and digestive system, and destroying them permits the passage of the stomach contents to the pulmonary cavity, or rather first the cadaveric softening of the esophagus is produced by perforations in the pleura. In such cases a brownish fluid with an acidic odor is found.

Liver: Upon cutting it, dark red fluid oozes out spontaneously or by pressure, with bubbles coming from vascular channels. The gaseous bubbles can be produced in a variable quantity, the organ thus acquiring a spongy aspect, or giving off foam from its dissected surface.

Stomach: its entrance and exit valves contract until closing; when relaxation begins, those valves and various sphincters open. The gastric content can empty out little by little toward the oral cavity, especially if the position of the corpse is changed; soon the auto-digestion of the stomach begins, from the effect of its own gastric juice or acid before death, so that under its effect the mucous membrane acquires a special transparency, until it disappears. The submucous membrane is also infiltrated and changes color until the muscular tissue finally softens and the wall disintegrates spontaneously or at the slightest contact, permitting the contents to pour into the peritoneal cavity where it continues to digest the surrounding fatty tissue.

Intestine: the walls of the intestine, stretched by the postmortal formation of gases, have a thin and pale appearance; the gases accumulate in the upper part of the intestine, whereas the blood flows downward to the lower part, accumulating most notably in the pelvis, which for this reason acquires a bluish coloration.

Male genital apparatus: the musculature of the cavity where the semen is lodged also experiences rigor mortis, because of which its contents passes into the urethra and can spill out through the penis.

Muscles: shortly after death, two or four hours later, rigor mortis sets in, which results in shortening and rigidity of the muscles. This is attributed, following the formation of acids, to the tissues' imbibing.

Skeleton: does not experience important changes; the actual putrefaction of the bone begins relatively late.

XV

Greta Garbo: (the famous ballerina has been a great success that night as the star of her ballet; back in her suite at the Grand Hotel in Berlin she wants to share her happiness but the eagerly awaited guest has not arrived; it is late, the orchestra in the main salon, floors below, has just retired) The music has stopped . . . how quiet it is tonight! . . . It was never so quiet in the Grand Hotel . . . (she looks at a bunch of flowers sent by admirers) These flowers make me think of funerals, don't they, Suzette?

The faithful companion: They're just lilies, Madame, . . . lilies.

Greta Garbo: Suzette . . . please ring the Baron. (the companion dials the number, the telephone rings but no one answers)

The faithful companion: It doesn't answer, Madame.

Greta Garbo: (not knowing that her lover Baron von Geigern lies murdered since the night before in that other room of the hotel) Ring, Suzette, ring . . . (to herself) Come to me, chéri . . . I'm longing for you. Last night I couldn't sleep, thinking that you might come to me . . .

(from *Grand Hotel*, Metro-Goldwyn-Mayer)

After a day's wait in Leopoldo Druscovich's apartment, Gladys Hebe D'Onofrio received the suitcase of clothes sent by her mother from White Beach. She couldn't give a tip to the delivery man because he didn't have change for the big bill Leo had left under the Toledan scissors. The first thing she took out of the suitcase was the bottle of sedatives, she had not been able to sleep the night before and needed a rest for her nerves. It was 6:23, hours before Leo had informed her on the telephone that the new nomination for São Paulo would appear in the 7 o'clock edition of an important evening newspaper. At approximately 7:25 the doorman would slip the newspaper under the door as he did every night, and at 10:30, according to Leo's arrangements, they were awaiting Gladys at an important party to give her a certain answer. Gladys thought that if she took the sedative now, she would become unnerved again when she read the newspaper and she would need an additional dose. Her mother had also sent her the curlers and all of her cosmetics. Gladys thought that putting on the curlers would calm her nerves, besides if she felt strong enough at night to go to the party her hair would only need to be brushed. She did the operation as slowly as possible, to cut short the wait for the newspaper. In fifteen minutes she finished with her hair and applied nutrient cream to her face. This only took ten minutes including the facial massage with her fingertips.

During that space of time her successive reasoning, in summary, was as follows: since she was not in a normal psychic condition to appear at São Paulo, Leo was right in disqualifying her; she would also probably not be in condition to confront the test that night, which consisted of attending a party at the house of the director of an important municipal gallery; that offer was only meant as compensation for her recent exclusion, that is, a charitable and not exactly professional act; her work, very probably, was a fraud; if her work had not been a fraud Leo Druscovich would have sent her to São Paulo; if her work was a fraud she would never exhibit it in public galleries, nor to friends either; if she did not exhibit her work she would not be able to earn money or apply for a grant; since her savings from the United States were fast diminishing, if she did not earn money with her artistic production she soon would have to take any old job; she would not have the strength to tackle any old job; since her mother's pension would surely not provide for all their expenses, Gladys would be forced to take any old job; the only activity that pleased her was her artistic work, but she had stopped believing in it, which prevented her from exhibiting it in public; if she found the strength to tackle any old job, she would only succeed in subsisting; subsisting would only prolong her present discomfort.

Once the facial massage was over, Gladys took the top off the bottle of sleeping pills and counted them. The resulting number, twelve, gave her occasion for some reasoning which, in summary, was as follows: twelve pills would not be enough to take one's life; if they weren't really enough she could open her veins with one of Leo's razor blades, there were probably some in the bathroom; even if feasible, that last method had disadvantages, since it was a slow and painful death, an unexpected visitor could come in and thwart the attempt; on the contrary it would be more certain and faster to jump out the window of that eighth floor, since throwing herself out head first the attempt could not fail; if she threw herself out head first, she would do it according to the instructions of the swimming teacher at a certain sports club, she should jump as she did when she dived into the pool as a little girl, but with the difference that on this occasion she would not place her arms in front protecting her head; if she decided to jump there was no sense waiting the half hour prescribed by cosmeticians to take off the nutrient cream once the massage with fingertips had been concluded, but if she already took off that cream and then didn't have the courage to jump out the window, her skin would be impaired at the party that night; on the contrary if she left the cream on for the prescribed half hour and before the time was up she could not restrain the urge to jump out the window, whoever picked her up on the street would notice the grotesque detail of the cream-covered face.

Gladys put the twelve pills back into the bottle and covered it. Immediately she opened it again. Her successive reasoning, in summary, was as follows: although twelve pills were not enough to destroy a healthy constitution, they were enough for hers, already near to being saturated with barbiturates; although that was probable, more certain would be the effect of the twelve pills mixed with an alcoholic beverage, as her upset two nights ago in Leo's car had indicated; if a rum cocktail had been enough for that prolonged fainting spell, there was no doubt that her constitution was seriously undermined by daily sedatives; although the mistreatment she had later received from Leo was unpardonable, it was logical that a man of his intelligence would be irritated by the eccentricities of a woman like her, depressed, one-eyed, and lacking real talent; since a rum cocktail had made her unconscious, twelve pills mixed with whiskey would undoubtedly cause her death; now then, if she had no talent at present, in the past however she had produced at least one work of quality, the one awarded a prize in the Fall Show, and she would have liked to have shown Leo that work, now the Museum's property and kept in some State warehouse; although her classmate the creator of the Icarus had not liked that small work, Leo might like it; if an artist manages to create one esthetically valid piece at some moment of her life, it is possible that she will create another one later on; although her last artistic experiment had failed, it was very possible that it wasn't inferior to María Esther Vila's conventional products; María Esther Vila's products did not deserve the name of experiments; if she'd had the strength she would have appeared before an audience to establish the difference between the work of one and the

203

other; even though the São Paulo audience was of a high international level, perhaps her work would be better understood by an audience that spoke the same language, with a background similar to hers, that is, Argentine; her best audience, then, would be Buenos Aires; if her best audience was Buenos Aires, she should go to the party that night and accept the proposal; if Leo had formulated the proposal it was because he was sure that she would reject it; if she finally dared to appear at the party, she would state that she had been disqualified for the personal and arguable reasons of one of the members of the jury; if she was really going to do that, it would be better to write it all on paper and read it there at the party, or fix clearly in her memory all the terms of the accusation, so as not to run the risk of being inhibited by shyness in front of all the people.

She looked for paper and pencil, but her attention span was not very steady. She heated a cup of coffee. She drank it in small sips, savoring it; she was forbidden to have coffee because it overexcited her. She looked for a formula with which to address those present at the party, she did not know where to begin, she could not think of any convincing introduction. She immediately felt a strong pressure on her temples and an accelerated pulse. She put down the pencil, threw herself on the bed. She looked at the clock, still forty minutes to go before the newspaper arrived. She considered the possibility of taking a sedative, immediately she decided against that because it would make her feel dazed at the party later on. She visualized the creator of the Icarus—whom she had not thought of for a long time—there in that room among Leo's belongings. She considered the possibility that he would look considerably aged, since he was older than she. She deduced that he must be almost forty years old. Gladys, without intending to, began to caress her vaginal lips, her pulse seemed to quiet down, she tried to remember in detail the physical traits of the creator of the Icarus, in twenty years she had forgotten some of them. Gladys did not experience

204

pleasurable sensations, barely some relief for her nerves, something to keep her hands busy. Sooner than expected she heard the sound of the newspaper being slipped under the door.

In the second section there was a square with the announcement of María Esther Vila's nomination as the Argentine representative in the São Paulo Bienal, without any reference to the previous candidate. Gladys read in the adjacent column the weekly program of the Colón theater's musical season—*Turandot*—, and on the same page articles on cultural activities. Her successive reasoning, in summary, was as follows: in spite of having wanted to very much, she had never seen Puccini's opera *Turandot,* and therefore it was possible that she would never see it; if she never got to see *Turandot,* she was even more unlikely to be able to attend the lecture series on Parapsychology which was announced for the following month at the university, thus losing the chance to investigate a field that interested her a lot; as to the important film premieres scheduled for that week, it was possible that she would never know if they were a success or a failure, but if she unexpectedly got to see the opera *Turandot* that would not only mean that she had managed to overcome the difficulties of that night but that she would also be able to see some of the aforementioned movies, which in any case she wouldn't prefer to other operas which were not scheduled for that week, although they were perhaps for the following month, even the following year; the number of operas which she had never seen and was interested in seeing was substantial, but more possible than seeing all of them was certainly that she would not see any of them; as to the automobile race which was announced in the last column, it was possible that she would never get to know the results; even in the case of overcoming the difficulties of that night, she would probably not find out the results the next day since car racing did not interest her; concerning the horoscope—the next day's, since it was the evening newspaper—, even if she didn't believe in the vague astrological commentaries of newspapers and magazines, that forecast could be considered correct, since they predicted for her sign, on the work level the tendency to react with unusual ardor which could be the reason for disputes, on the emotional level the tendency toward instability, on the financial level difficulties due to the expectation of excessive gains, and for corollary, flexibility was prescribed as the rule of the day; if that forecast could be considered correct, it meant that the following day would be as difficult as the one she was now living.

She noticed that there was still a trace of slime on her right hand, she went to the bathroom and while she waited for it to run hot water she looked inside the medicine chest. Shaving brush, cream, and electric razor; she concluded that if Leo wanted to shave with his own equipment instead of going to his barber he would have to return there. She washed her hands but felt a slight trace of sweat in her armpits; she decided to take a shower and eliminate all dirt. The hot water produced a pleasant effect, the strong spurt from the shower took the place of a massage. Gladys felt the desire to wet her head as well, to feel the powerful stream on the back of her neck. But if she wet her head all the care put into waving her hair and nourishing her skin would be wasted. With nervous movements she took off the curlers, she didn't know if after the shower she would put them in again or not. With toilet paper she abruptly took off the nutrient cream, scraping her skin. The hot water brought her immediate pleasure, she decided to leave her head under the stream several minutes, the pressure on the back of her neck and temples seemed to subside.

While she dried herself she was forced to decide if she should put in the curlers or not. She decided to first lie down for a few minutes on the bed; so as not to wet the pillow she wrapped her head in a towel. She lay down, immediately remembered that on one occasion Leo had entered her hotel room and had found her with a towel tied around her head. Her skin was now free of all secretions, she passed her hand along her shoulders, she had the impression that her skin was soft and inviting. She closed her eyes and tried to remember how that meeting with Leo had been, and at what moment the towel had fallen off her head. She could not control a strong desire to masturbate. A quick, forceful orgasm came on, she had succeeded in visualizing Leo penetrating her and smiling at her sweetly, something which he had done simultaneously only the morning before, in the presence of María Esther.

Gladys breathed deeply, she expected to sleep at least an hour, as usually happened after every masturbatory act. She thought that she would not need sedatives to relax before the party. It was necessary for her to sleep, without that she knew that she would not be able to carry out any plan. She tried to relax, several minutes passed, in her legs and arms persistent nervous discharges began to occur. She changed position several times, they were all uncomfortable. She blamed the pillow, much softer than her usual one. The pressure on her skull and the back of her neck began to sneak up on her, and gradually increased. Gladys suddenly detected the cause: coffee. It had always produced that effect on her, she concluded that the discomfort would become greater and would turn into a migraine headache, properly speaking, especially on this occasion, after a sleepless night. She remembered that masturbation always produced headaches if she didn't go to sleep right away, to which the effect of the coffee was now added. She looked at the time, it was 7:47, two and a half hours later she should be at the party. The quickest solution was the sedative, but it would make her sleepy, under its effect she would not be clearheaded in front of all those people. She considered a glass of whiskey, that might counteract the coffee. She poured a generous measure, prepared to drink it in one gulp when the telephone rang.

She thought it would be Leo, who would communicate something pleasant, and might even tell her something important, something equivalent to a solution to all her problems, which would prevent her from drinking that alcohol she so much disliked. But that didn't happen, from the other end of the line came a shy and extremely polite female voice asking to speak with Leo. Gladys answered, dryly, that he wasn't in. Whoever was calling earnestly asked to let Leo know that they were waiting for some money for a needy family, money which had been promised and had still not arrived. Gladys assured her that she would relay the message, hung up without saying good-by and immediately afterwards drank the whiskey straight in a few sips. She felt a pleasant warmth in her chest but no symptoms of sleep. She served herself another measureful, almost double. She drank it, and very soon her eyelids felt heavy. She finally fell asleep. She dreamed that she had to get up to go somewhere, lazily she would get up, stop the alarm clock, get dressed, and arrive on time at her job in New York. The dream was repeated several times, on each occasion the effort to get up and stop the alarm clock became greater.

Gladys woke up at 3:12 in the morning. Her headache was almost unbearable. She looked at the clock, upon seeing the time she realized she could no longer go to the aforementioned party, and her successive reasoning, in summary, was as follows: since it was impossible to attend the important party, she wouldn't go anywhere else that night; she wouldn't go anywhere that night or ever again; she would stay there until someone came to get her and take her anywhere; if it were possible she would never again bother anybody with requests; if she did not make any decisions, that meant that excluded from her behavior would be irreparable measures such as suicide, an act which would make her mother and even Leo grief-stricken; if she gave up all activity she would remain in her mother's care for whom, almost certainly, it would be a pastime to take care of her; she wouldn't go anywhere, she would not move from the cottage, and if her mother died the daughter would not accompany the coffin to the White Beach cemetery, she would remain motionless in her bed, where she would die because no one would bring her anything to eat.

The night was very quiet, one could not hear traffic on the street. Gladys sharpened her hearing because of a slight noise that she could not locate. It came from the next apartment, beyond the wall where the largest picture hung. It sounded like ohs and sighs from a woman. Gladys got up and stuck her ear against the wall. A woman was moaning from excessive pleasure, her partner was murmuring unintelligible words to her. Once in a while one even heard the squeak of a bed's coil spring. Gladys moved away a few inches, one heard only the higher pitched voice, and very faintly. She stuck her ear against the wall again and could distinctly hear the deeper voice and the noise of the bedspring. Gladys felt an overbearing desire to be in that man's arms. The ohs increased, Gladys waited for the orgasm to provoke even more audible exclamations, but the crescendo stopped. One could barely hear a nasal murmur. Gladys guessed the cause, he was drowning her indiscreet moans with kisses.

During the silence which followed, Gladys' reasoning, in summary, was as follows: while only a few inches away a woman was seized by immense pleasure, she herself was putting up with, among other things, a bad headache, the displeasure of Leo's abandonment, the disqualification by the jury, and the threat of innumerable headaches which awaited her in White Beach; if such inequalities of luck were possible, she could not find any reason why the less favorable should fall to her; if she had the less favorable luck, she did not find any reason why she should accept it; what's more, if unknown powers had decided that she was to have the less favorable luck, she did not find any reason to be their accomplice; if those unknown powers were committing a cruel injustice, those powers were reproachable; any complicity with those powers made her reproachable as well; in the case of continuing to live, she would not be able to avoid future complicity with the aforementioned powers; the very fact of continuing to live

209

made her their accomplice; even if saying good-by to her mother telephonically would be painful for the latter, she could not think of a better solution; even if it would take effort, it was necessary to talk to her mother clearly and calmly; even if the farewell would be sad, in the end her disappearance would be a relief for the one who would thus be able to again take up her activities as an oral reader.

She made a call to her mother's neighbors in White Beach. The operator informed her of a ten-minute delay. She decided to cover herself, she did not want to be found naked on the sidewalk, she put on a brassiere and underpants and her nightgown over that. The ten minutes over, she demanded to be put through and they informed her that the lines were interrupted by bad weather on the coast. She happily cancelled the call, since she would never again hear her mother's voice. She was surprised to notice that the headache was going away. She turned on a faucet in the bathroom, the water came out very cool, she drank several sips from the palm of her hand. Lastly she considered the possibility of having her dark glasses on when she jumped out the window, but she presumed that during her body's course through the air the glasses would come off and fall separately. Even if those glasses were somewhat deteriorated and lately she used them with some apprehension since they seemed out of style, she had affection for them, because she had been using them since the emptying of her eye. Leaving them there would seem an act of ingratitude; she decided to hold them tightly in her hand, so as not to lose them during the fall. The headache had passed almost completely, she thought with relief that it was the last one in her life. She went to the window, opened it, the small balcony had a railing barely a yard high.

XVI

Rita Hayworth: (dazzling in her gauze negligée with a revealing neckline, but profoundly disturbed since she has just found out that her husband's new bodyguard is none other than the only man she ever loved in her life and by whom she was abandoned; she talks trying to hide it all) It's been a pleasure to meet you, Mister Farrell.

Her gangster husband: (in a tone of affectionate protest) But Gilda . . . his name is Johnny.

Rita Hayworth: (gaily) I'm sorry! Johnny is a very difficult name to remember . . . and so easy to forget.

(from *Gilda,* Columbia Pictures)

Buenos Aires, May 23, 1969

The young wife could not suppress vocal expressions corresponding to her pleasure. The husband, stimulated, did his best to keep up his performance. During brief seconds he doubled his attacks but suddenly upon reducing the speed of his movements to a minimum, he made a felicitous erotic discovery. The young wife remembered movie scenes projected in slow motion and adapted the activity of her hands which moved over her husband's back

211

to the same pace; she thought maintaining silence would reinforce the otherworldliness of that moment. Very slowly he withdrew the member as far as the vaginal lips and then in the same manner again inserted it totally. After a few minutes the young wife could not restrain herself any longer and again panted and sighed explosively. The husband suggested that she lower the volume of her exclamations because they might wake up the baby who slept in the next room. She answered that nothing would wake him up since he had drunk his whole bottle and would not need another one for three hours. She uttered new sighs, which did not succeed in totally covering a noise coming from the neighboring apartment. More precisely, what they had heard was a kind of brushing against the wall which separated the apartments and against which the marriage bed was placed. The possibility that someone might hear them increased the couple's excitement and rushed the orgasm. The husband clapped his mouth over hers and thus stifled all the climactic sounds. On his way to the bathroom he looked at the electric clock in the kitchen, it was 3:31 and at 5 he had to be at the airport. Before leaving he asked his wife if she really didn't need anything from Paraguay since between the time of the plane's arrival and the time to return to the cockpit he would have a moment to wander around the stores at the airport in search of something useful at a good price. She considered any purchase a superfluous luxury, at that moment all her wishes were fulfilled. She preferred not to get out of bed, she excused herself for not helping him. The husband's clothes were all ready and the overnight bag was packed, she had taken care of all the details before going to bed. She added that by staying in bed she could hold onto his warmth.

Now ready to say good-by, with the bag in one hand and the cap of his uniform in the other, he bent down to kiss her. He passed the cap to his left hand that was already holding the bag and with the right caressed her pubis, under the flowered towel that covered it. His wife asked him to drive carefully, it had drizzled during the night and the streets would be slippery. When left alone she tried to sleep. A few minutes later she heard an abrupt screeching of brakes on the street, she quickly threw on her bathrobe and went out on the balcony to see if what she feared most in the world had happened. It was a false alarm, two unknown vehicles had met head on but they were already on their way again; also witness to the scene was a woman peering out of the next balcony. The young wife was at first startled, but, full of curiosity to know who her eccentric neighbor's visitor was, she greeted her. As soon as the woman looked straight at her, fearfully, she was recognized. The young wife was able to identify her immediately by the defect in the right eye. She told her, without realizing that it implied a reference to the particular mark, that the neighbor had spoken to her and her husband at length about his discovery at the seashore, and added that she felt honored to meet someone of her talent. The woman did not ask how she had been able to recognize her, she smiled forcibly and could not manage to say a word. They heard the telephone ring in the eccentric neighbor's apartment, the woman excused herself, she had to answer the call. The young wife said she would remain on the balcony a few minutes, and she would wait for her so that they could talk a little more, she added with halting words that she was very interested in chatting with someone different, a promising artist. The woman barely smiled and went in, she left the window open.

The young wife managed to hear the woman assuring the telephone operator of having cancelled that call before. The woman hung up the receiver but did not immediately return to the balcony. The young wife reconsidered and decided to go back to bed, but since it would be difficult for her to get back to sleep, she would first drink a cup of milk. She said softly "good night, ma'am." She didn't hear an answer, became uncomfortable, she thought that the least a normally educated person could do was to respond. Immediately she thought that the woman

213

might be upset, she looked bad, the open eye expressed anguish, it was bloodshot. The young wife called again, louder, "miss," she said this time. The woman returned to the balcony, had on her dark glasses.

She looked at the young wife without speaking, with a slight smile. The young wife asked her if she didn't feel well; the other, evasive, in turn inquired why the neighbor had spoken of her existence. The young wife answered that Leo often came to talk to them because he suffered from insomnia, the couple was often up at night because of odd flight schedules, trying to sleep during the day if the baby let them. The young wife suggested that she join her in a glass of milk with cake, a pound cake that she herself had made. Instead of answering, the woman again asked about Leo's references to her. The young wife repeated the invitation, adding that milk helped one to sleep and thus she could tell her how interested she and her husband had been in Leo's stories, her husband had even regretted that São Paulo was not on his flight list for the following month, if not he would have been able to attend the artist's show at that exhibition.

The woman asked what kind of job the husband had, the answer was that he worked as a radio operator on international flights. The young wife looked at the cloudy sky and said that she would never get used to the risks involved in constant flying. The woman tried to comfort her saying that there was more danger below where they were, submerged in the pollution of the modern world, than up in the air. The young wife said that she knew that well, she paused and added that her mother had died three years back of a heart attack, after working a long time as a telephone operator in an airless booth. She could not prevent tears from coming to her eyes, the woman said that she was very sorry, in turn paused and added that she would accept the invitation extended.

When the woman entered the neighboring home the young wife said shyly that Leo could come too, if he was there next door. The woman said that he wasn't there, he had just left her the apartment for several days, he had to leave the city. The young wife begged her to talk in a whisper so as not to wake up the child and showed her a picture of her husband in uniform, a young man with a pleasant physique and nice expression on his face. The woman looked attentively at the picture, then looked around at the walls and decorations, came closer to a picture frame where the young wife was with her husband on their wedding day. The young wife went to get the milk and pound cake, meanwhile the woman looked quickly at the unmade bed, the towel thrown on the floor, and on a chair, large-sized pajamas. The woman even had time to look again at the picture of the young man in uniform. The woman asked if the mother's sudden death had made her very apprehensive. The young wife said yes, she constantly thought of the possibility of losing her husband in an accident, or her baby for numerous causes, mainly falls, or food poisoning. She added that she was less afraid of epidemics since the baby was duly vaccinated, and in general her spells of insomnia had their origin in those negative thoughts, even though—it is necessary to clarify—those depressed states came up only in her husband's absence.

The woman said that the pound cake was to her liking. The young wife served her another portion and offered her a sleeping pill. The woman asked her if she were going to take one too. The young wife said no, because then the baby would wake up before the mother. The woman also rejected the pill, her face seemed to cloud up again and she got up to go. The young wife begged her to stay longer, that way they could talk about the art shows for which she was certainly preparing, following São Paulo. The woman answered very softly that she didn't know, there was a silence, the woman squeezed her lips still tighter. The young wife inquired about the possibility of an exhibit in Buenos Aires. The woman answered that there was a possibility, but unfortunately that night she had not appeared at a party where the matter would have

215

been discussed. The young wife indiscreetly asked why she had been absent. The woman answered that she had not felt well. The young wife said that the next time that happened she could call her, since she spent most of the day alone with her child, and even at night she could call her, if she saw light from the balcony. The woman explained, looking in the other direction, that perhaps the next day she would no longer be staying there.

The young wife got up to go to the kitchen to fetch more milk, she had noticed that the woman was not touching the second portion of cake and attributed that to the fact that there was no more liquid left to accompany it, but upon returning she saw that the woman was standing beside the exit door. The young wife thought that it was no longer fitting to insist and offered her the piece of cake to take with her and eat with breakfast. The woman opened the door, didn't answer, only smiled slightly. The young wife's telephone rang. She asked the woman to come in again for a moment and to close the door behind her. The call was from the husband, he was already at the airport and wanted to know if in the meantime she hadn't thought of something she wanted from Paraguay. The young wife answered no; although perhaps the visitor might want something, next explaining to the husband who it was. The husband said to invite her to dinner that night, he would return at three in the afternoon and would have time to take a nap. The young woman asked the visitor if she wanted some North American product on sale in Paraguay. The visitor hesitated a second and answered no. The husband asked to have the visitor come to the phone so that he could offer her the service personally. They conversed for a few minutes, the young man's voice sounded lively, almost adolescent, and projected a sincere enthusiasm to meet that personality of the Argentine art world.

The conversation had barely ended when they heard the child cry; the voices and the ringing of the telephone had awakened him. The young mother excused herself, she would leave the visitor alone for a few minutes because she had to go up to the roof, where she had forgotten she had diapers hanging on the line. The woman remained alone, looked toward the balcony, where the access door had remained open. The child continued crying. The woman did not go into the next room to see him, instead she went to the bathroom, checked the medicine chest and found a container of contraceptive cream concealed behind the package of cotton. She took the cover off to smell it. She covered it again and left it in its place, duly concealed by the package of cotton. From there she went to the marriage bed. She pulled the top sheet all the way down, two black curly hairs appeared, attributable to the pubic zone. She returned the sheet to its place. She looked around, the man's pajamas were still lying on a chair. The visitor looked them over, smelled the shirt and then the pants.

Sounds could be heard in the hallway, the young wife reappeared with the diapers, dampened by the drizzle; she lit the oven in the kitchen and placed them there. She apologized for her delay and for the annoyance caused by the child's crying. The young mother took him in her arms and showed him to the visitor, moreover she asked her if she and her husband had decided on the phone exactly what time they would get together for dinner. The visitor looked at the child as if she had never seen one in her life, she answered that the young man had requested before hanging up that the two of them arrange the details; then she was silent. The young mother was ready to make any comment to avoid silence when the visitor, with a louder voice than was usual in her, asked that dinner be as late as possible, because she intended to first talk to the director of a certain municipal gallery, and she didn't know when he would receive her in his office; she added that the child was beautiful. The young mother said that she had to change the baby immediately, and again offered the visitor another glass of milk to accompany the slice of cake already cut. The visitor unexpectedly accepted. The young mother was even more surprised when the latter asked her for a sleeping pill. As if ashamed the woman explained that even though she had drank too much that night, many hours had already passed and there wouldn't be any conflict at all between alcohol and barbiturates. She swallowed the pill with a sip of milk. The young mother took the already dry diapers out of the oven, laid them flat on the marriage bed and put the child there. She asked the visitor to sit next to her so that she wouldn't turn her back on the visitor during the operation and begged to hear about her artistic plans, but she immediately corrected herself, since the visitor should talk about that during dinner and she wanted to avoid repetitions that would be boring for the artist. The young mother instead asked her to talk about the things that frightened her. The visitor, seated at the head of the bed and with her head resting against the headboard of padded silk, said that storms frightened her. The young woman did not allow her visitor to continue the enumeration, she began to talk about her own fears, mainly one, the aforementioned loss of her dear ones. She explained that, as for herself, she wasn't afraid of death but she was terrified by the death of those she loved. While she was saying this she noticed that the visitor's hair seemed sticky and could therefore leave grease on the silk of the headboard. With the excuse of offering her more comfort she placed, with affectionate good manners but without asking permission, a pillow between the head and the delicate headboard.

Next she told the circumstances of her mother's death. The visitor looked at her, seemed to be comfortably settled. The narration abounded in details of profound sadness. The child, relieved of the rashes on his backside by the talcum powder and his mother's caresses, smiled. The young wife spoke without looking at the visitor, attentive to the care of the child. At one moment she asked the visitor something and didn't receive an answer. She looked at her and only then noticed that she had fallen asleep. She turned off the ceiling light and turned on the nightlamp on the side opposite that occupied by the visitor. Her sleep

218

was doubtlessly serene, since her breathing flattened and swelled her chest evenly. But the young mother, always fearful of fatal accidents, thought that the visitor might have fainted, or suffered a heart attack, or some other terrible mishap. She tried to take her pulse, but could not find any vein. There was no way out but to shake the woman, her dark glasses fell on the floor; the young mother placed them on the night table. The woman woke up, smiled slightly and excused herself. She sat up halfway, the young mother told her that if she wanted she could stay and sleep there. The visitor could not contain a wide yawn. The young mother insisted that she could sleep with her and the baby in that bed, which was wide enough. The visitor answered that it would be too much bother, but did not stand up, she remained sitting on the bed. The young mother assured her that they would sleep well, she would even take advantage of the fact that the baby was awake to give him the next bottle, so that he wouldn't wake them up until late in the morning. The visitor accepted by merely tilting her head, the slight smile remained on her lips. The young woman suggested placing the pillow in a normal position, for everybody's comfort. The visitor went back to sleep almost immediately. The young mother returned to the child, he clapped hands and upon smiling displayed two tiny teeth. Two graceful dimples formed on the corners of his mouth. His skin was rosy, his blue eyes light, his hair curly and blond. The young wife then looked at the woman asleep and thought how marvelous it would have been if her mother were still alive. Her eyes filled with tears, her mother had died before the child's birth, she had not even known her husband, barely a suitor at the time of her demise. She closed her eyes and thought of him. She still felt a pleasant sensation of warmth in her vagina, and further up a slight burning. She wondered if inside her a new being wasn't about to bud, she decided that if it was a girl she would name her after her dead mother.

219

ABOUT THE AUTHOR

Manuel Puig was born in 1932 in a small town in the Argentine pampas. He studied philosophy at the University of Buenos Aires, and in 1956 he won a scholarship from the Italian Institute in Buenos Aires and chose to pursue studies in film direction at the Cinecitta in Rome. There he worked as an assistant director until 1962, when he began to write his first novel. Puig's novels—*Betrayed by Rita Hayworth, Heartbreak Tango, The Buenos Aires Affair,* and *Kiss of the Spider Woman*—have been translated into fourteen languages. Now living in New York City, Puig has taught at City College, and, commencing in September 1980, will teach at Columbia University.